More praise for *Paris in the Twentieth Century*

"Verne's canny predictions of certain technological wonders, as well as his portrayal of the dominance of finance and technology in the modern world, are prescient indeed."

—*The Seattle Times*

"Verne's early novel has at last been published, and it offers a unique reading experience for the modern science fiction reader."

—*The Orlando Sentinel*

"A true collector's item, an important piece of literature . . . *Paris in the Twentieth Century* is a surprising and disturbingly accurate rendering of society's quest for perfection. In order to achieve perfection, Verne points out, we must sacrifice our own individuality, and inevitably, fall prey to automation. The adult in me sits in awe of Verne's amazing predictions in this lost novel. The child inside is rekindled with new warmth of getting reacquainted with an old friend thought long dormant on my bookshelf. Welcome to the Twentieth Century, Mr. Verne."

—J. C. Patterson
The Clarion-Ledger

"Remarkably, Verne's 20th-century Paris rarely seems dated. This may be because Verne was uncannily correct in his major predictions, that the future would be dominated by corporations and that technology would be the dominant god. Nothing impractical or unprofitable can exist in this world, and, in the end, people are no more than fragile machines expected to serve without question the corporate deities. . . . A welcome—and startling—curiosity."

—*Kirkus Reviews*

Paris in the Twentieth Century

Paris in the
Twentieth Century

JULES VERNE

TRANSLATED BY RICHARD HOWARD
INTRODUCTION BY EUGEN WEBER

BALLANTINE BOOKS • NEW YORK

A Del Rey® Book
Published by Ballantine Books

http://www.randomhouse.com/delrey/

Library of Congress Catalogue Card Number: 97-94115

Illustrations by Anders Wenngren

ISBN: 978-0-345-42039-8

Book design by Wynn Dan
Cover illustration by Mark Burkhardt

Manufactured in the United States of America

First Ballantine Books Edition: November 1997

O terrible influence of this race
which serves neither god nor king,
given over to the mundane sciences,
to base mechanical professions!
Pernicious breed! What will you not
attempt, left to your own devices,
abandoned without restraint to that
fatal spirit of knowledge, of
invention, of progress.

PAUL-LOUIS COURIER (1772–1825)

(from *Lettres au Rédacteur du Censeur*)

When I was eleven, my mother (twice divorced) re-married, and we moved into my stepfather's house. He was her first cousin, and their marriage was designed to be one of comfort and familiarity, yet the partners to it had neglected to acknowledge one shared flaw, which soon became a distressing factor in our family life. Both husband and wife were raring, tearing alco-holics, from whom I took a sort of aggressive refuge in a set of olive leather books I had found on a shelf over the piano. The twelve double volumes of *The Works of Jules Verne* became my imaginative life while all hell was breaking loose around me. I lived in them, utterly dissolved in the Splendors and Miseries of Technology, reading with an intensity probably doubled because of the chaos those big visions protected me from.

I have translated this newly discovered first novel, which Verne wrote when he was thirty-five, as a ges-ture of gratitude for all those hours of rescue work, from which I am still profiting. No space machine of

Verne's peculiar invention was more powerful than those books of his, no intraterrestrial vehicle more effective in promoting total (and saving) absorption. Much of the old spell—more diagrammatic, less suavely joined—abides in *Paris in the Twentieth Century,* and I am delighted to be artisanally connected with this story of tragic anticipations, a dystopia which now seems as familiar to us as that old gothic romance the Return of the Repressed. It is scary to discover, reading Verne, that one's future is also one's past, but it certainly makes for an enthralling reminder that the anticipation of a world is inevitably the myth of an eternal return.

RICHARD HOWARD

New York, March 1995

CONTENTS

Translater's Note vii

Introduction xi

Eugen Weber

"Citizens, can you imagine the future? City streets flooded with light . . . nations brothers . . . no more events. All will be happy." That is Victor Hugo in *Les Misérables,* published in 1862. In 1863 a much younger man sat down to imagine the future and, though full of marvels, his version looks less happy by far. At thirty-five, Jules Verne had tried several trades and apparently mastered none—at least, not one that could ensure a stable income. *Five Weeks in a Balloon,* the tale that made his name, was just published, but fame still hung around the corner for the determined scribbler who dreamt of a literary career. So, the pages Jules Verne penned in 1863 to be revealed nearly 130 years later read very differently from the science fiction that we expect from him.

Avid reader of Edgar Allan Poe, Verne had been fascinated by the American's fantasies, seared by his scorn for American society and for the idea of progress. *Paris in the Twentieth Century* applies Poe's views to contemporary France, where poetry wages a losing battle against material reality. The Jules Verne we know from his "Extraordinary Voyages" translates the romantic exoticism of his youth onto a scientific (and didactic) plane. The Verne that we encounter here translates Romantic pessimism into social satire. In classic Jules Verne adventures the environment is there to be mastered; in twentieth century Paris it can only be suffered, and the narrative offers less entertaining description than cultural criticism.

The material setting is prescient and prophetic. There are electric lights in profusion; boulevards and department stores lit as brightly as the sun; gigantic hotels; great avenues filled with horseless carriages powered by internal combustion; noiseless gas cabs that turn corners and climb slopes with none of the problems of horses; public transport provided by street cars and automatic driverless trains; majestic mansions fitted with elevators and electric buttons that open doors; financial hives equipped with copiers, calculators, and fax machines. The capital city has become a great seaport, "a Liverpool in the heart of France," crowded with liners and freighters, whilst (only yards from where the Eiffel Tower went up in 1889) an electric lighthouse five hundred feet high looms over a forest of flag-studded masts.

Paris in the twentieth century—and, more specifically, in 1960—teems with prodigies that were hard to imagine a hundred years before; yet Jules Verne imagined them because the science and technology of his day suggested their possibility. Imagination is the capacity to rearrange available data or to extrapolate from them, and Verne was a masterful extrapolator. Work on the Suez Canal had begun in 1859: if seagoing ships could cross the desert with help from engineers, they could certainly sail up the Seine. The prototypes of internal combustion engines and of fax machines had been developed in 1859, the first Otis elevator ascended in New York in 1857, the first transatlantic cable would be laid in 1866, the first underground railway opened in London in 1862. Paris got one in 1900, but Jules Verne envisaged an elevated railway in the American style, powered by compressed air. Electrified streetcars appeared in the United States in the 1880s, in Europe in the 1890s. Even the electric chair that Verne's protagonist stumbles across as he roams through the Paris night would be inaugurated in New York State a quarter of a century later.

So Jules Verne's 1960 is neither unimaginable in 1860, nor unbelievable for today's readers. And Michel Dufrénoy, his hero, fits the period well. With his long hair, his literary aspirations, his rejection of the existing order and of a paying job, and his rather mopey manner, he prefigures the dreamy dropouts of the 1960s. Jules Verne's only child, a son born in 1861, was also named Michel; so were the ships that Jules loved to sail. We may assume that, in the author's eye, Michel is a positive figure. Yet one could say of him what Adolphe Thiers, the acerbic politician, said of Napoleon III: "He confuses the verb to dream with the verb to think." In fact, Michel is a fool, but a nice fool: a poet and a ninny, as one is entitled to be at sixteen; and sometimes at sixty. And his Paris, the one Jules Verne envisions for our century, is a ship of fools running onto the rocks of modernity.

Under Napoleon III, the great emperor's nephew who ruled France between 1848 and 1870, the country's industrial production doubled, and its communications network tripled. Business and government enterprise, notably, transformed Paris: wide straight streets, green parks and squares, new apartment buildings, monumental railway stations, and workers' housing on the outskirts for people displaced from the center of town. Verne noted the ferocious materialism of his time and anticipated the fallout of progress with anxious fascination: overpopulation, pollution, lodgings hard to find in a city center where offices and public buildings crowded out private dwellings, and everywhere "machines advantageously replacing human hands."

So many aspects of Jules Verne's imaginary twentieth century apply to the real one in which we live! The French language is in dire straits: specialists create their own jargon, scientists adopt English, *Franglais* is about to pounce. As with speech, so with social institutions: the family tends to self-destruction, marriage looks like heroic futility, the number of legitimate children diminishes, illegitimacy soars, bastards "form an impressive majority." Books still exist; indeed, since the invention of paper made of wood pulp (1851), there are more of them. More books but fewer readers: literature has been marginalized, and "knowledge is imparted by mechanical means." Mechanics have also invaded the arts. Music knows no more melody, painting no form, poetry sings *Electric Harmonies* and *Decarbonated Odes*, truly popular literature deals with practical matters like *Stress Theory* or *The Lubrication of Driveshafts*. Even Jules Verne failed to imagine that ideal warehouse for modern art, the Beaubourg museum, let alone the beau-bourgeoisie that worships at art's altars; nor had anyone yet coined words like "technocracy" and "technocrats." But the government of the Second Empire was heavily involved in intellectual and cultural life, patronage and administrative manipulation subsidized and suggested, "joining the useful to the disagreable" even more perhaps than they do today.

The Great Dramatic Warehouse (Chapter XIV), where Michel finds a job, houses teams of scribblers writing to order, or rewriting past successes as in Hollywood, to amuse "docile audiences by harmless works." "Abandon originality all ye who enter here!" could easily be engraved above its gate. What had begun as private enterprise had passed under control of the State and of its bureaucrats. Theatre managers (Verne had been one in his youth) became civil servants, authors state employees, and the stern censorship of nineteenth century administrations waned because self-censorship left no need for it.

Jules Verne's irony is sometimes heavy-handed. It can also be hard to discern for readers unaware of issues that concerned his times. Thus, unlike Britain, Belgium, or Prussia, the France of the first half of the nineteenth century had no national banking system; and this created problems in raising capital, obtaining credit, or even paying bills over a distance. In 1852, France joined the modern age when two visionary believers in industrial development and technocratic planning, the brothers Pereire, founded a national bank, the Crédit Mobilier, soon imitated by other joint stock clearing banks founded over the next ten years or so: Crédit Industriel, Crédit Foncier, Crédit Lyonnais. . . . The Academic Credit Union that appears in Chapter I transposes this financial revolution to the educational field: centralization, investment, profit, on a new mass scale. Verne's story begins on the Union's prize-giving day, a ceremony as familiar to the French of the 1860s as to their present-day descendants, and as commencement is to us. An educational system founded as the economy was, on competition, stimulated ambition by official recognition: prizes, medals, certificates of excellence, without which children were not expected to exert themselves. The struggle to win school prizes prepared for more serious struggles after graduation, hence for success in life. So the annual prize-giving day was a great occasion, and the speeches that marked it reflected values that society sought to inculcate: in this case, respect for foreign languages and for applied science.

In the 1860s, educated Frenchmen (few women had access to secondary education till later in the century) learnt to write good French by imitating models found in Latin and in the great authors of seventeenth and eighteenth century literature. That was the basis of rhetoric, whose models drawn from Greek and Roman antiquity taught good taste, elegant discourse, nobility of thought and of expression. Democratic opponents of rhetoric rejected it as pedantic, pompous, boring, and elitist. Victor Hugo, much admired by Michel as by Michel's creator, had recently denounced

Merchants of Greek! Merchants of Latin! pedants! dogs! Philistines! magisters! I hate you pedagogs.

But Hugo was in exile for opposition to the Empire, and the respectable classes respected the classical curriculum that he criticized.

More dangeous for rhetoric's fortunes, its teachings were out of tune with the times. "Fine words do not produce beet sugar, Alexandrine verse does not help extract sodium from sea salt," the physicist François Arago contended, attacking scholastic insistence on the classics and other useless knowledge. Michel Dufrénoy's prize for Latin verse brands him as an anachronism condemned to the same uselessness and rejection as his beloved teacher of rhetoric; and Verne's opening chapter joins in a debate that would not be resolved until 1902, when rhetoric was dropped from the curriculum.

Science, too, stood at the center of educational debates under a Second Empire which sought to encourage studies that would orient the young towards careers in useful industry. A degree in letters was more prestigious; but scientific training, the Emperor's Minister of Education asserted, would provide the non-commissioned officers of the industrial army. "Honor the concrete!" Let modern languages replace dead ones, let geography and modern history prepare young minds for contemporary living. Imperial lycées introduced "industrial classes" that did not call for Latin, offered commercial courses, installed laboratories and "electromagnetic apparatus." By the beginning of the twentieth century more students preferred "modern humanities" to the classics; by 1962 twice as much time was spent on the sciences, three times as much on modern languages, as in the century past. For a long time, however, the numbers involved remained pitifully small. In 1860 the national secondary system taught 35,000 students; in 1930, 67,000. Nevertheless, in the end Jules Verne proved right. By 1960 their number had risen to 343,000—more than double the Academic Credit Union's awesome 157,000; and only a few years later they passed the half million mark.

Extrapolating from the present can lead to error or to oversight. Fictional Parisians of the 1960s use copiers, calculators, and fax machines, but know no typewriters or even steel-nibbed pens. The bankers Michel hates write with quills, and keep accounts in a

Great Ledger inscribed in a fine hand by a calligrapher. Even Jules Verne's imagination needed a starting point; and typewriters, invented in 1867, patented in 1868—in the United States, of course—were simply not envisaged when he wrote. In the same vein, our author conceives garments of spun metal, but not the polyesters that chemical industry developed later; a bookstore like a warehouse, but no access to merchandise, stacks, or shelves; a multipurpose piano that can be used as bed, dresser, and commode, but not a world where servants do not serve at table.

All nations would be brothers, Hugo had predicted, and Verne agreed because the world had become one market and the links of commerce drew nations ever closer (Chapter VII). "No more events," meant no more sensational or discomforting happenings; no more wars, revolutions, crises; no more of what Verne called infernal politics. "All will be happy," Hugo had concluded. One has to doubt whether Verne agreed. Still, some of his forecasts brought grist to Hugo's mill. In Jules Verne's 1960s politics have withered and, since gazettes were about politics, not news, nobody bothers to read the press: "journalism has had its day." So have medicine which ran out of diseases, and lawyers who, now, would rather settle than go to court. Worst of the book's errors, war has vanished, armies are no more, armies of businessmen have replaced them. "When soldiers become mechanics, wars become ridiculous." Would it were so. Jules Verne could not know that, by the time he died, the budget of industry and commerce accounted for 1.7 percent of national expenses, the Army for 23.4 percent. He could not know but, surely, might have guessed.

When Jules Verne died in 1904, at seventy-seven, his world fame was a little worn, his name on a title page no longer sold books like hot cakes. But for two or three decades after his first triumph in 1863 with *Five Weeks in a Balloon,* few French novelists, if any, enjoyed comparable world success. A bestseller in his lifetime, with 1.6 million copies of his French editions sold by 1904 and still more after his death, he remains the most translated of French authors: 224 translations in twenty-three countries.

Son of a comfortable provincial family, the lad grew up in Nantes, the great port on the Loire, studied law as his lawyer father wanted, but soon followed his literary inclinations into the theatre, writing comedies and operettas (one with music by Offenbach), then helping to manage the theatre founded by his friend and patron, Alexandre Dumas. Married in 1857, he bought into a financial agency, worked as a broker on the Stock Exchange, but continued to write poems, stories, lyrics, and plays until Dumas introduced him to his own publisher, Pierre-Jules Hetzel, editor of Balzac, Hugo, Baudelaire, and George Sand, who was to serialize and edit the sixty-four-volume series of Verne's "Extraordinary Voyages" over some forty years.

After the triumph of *Five Weeks*, Hetzel offered Jules Verne a contract for three books a year, paid roughly at the same rate that he paid George Sand, and also hired him as a regular contributor to a young people's magazine, the *Review of Education and Recreation*, where many of Verne's novels would be published in serial form. The theatrical experience was not wasted either, for the storyteller adapted many of his novels for the stage, notably *Around the World in Eighty Days* (1874), *The Children of Captain Grant* (1878), *Michel Strogoff* (1880), and a number of others. Since theatre was the cinema of those days, the success of his plays increased both fame and revenues; whilst, unsurprisingly, one of the first French films made, in 1902, took as its subject an 1865 adventure, *From the Earth to the Moon*, whose original subtitle read: "A direct crossing in 97 hours and 20 minutes."

With a steady income assured, the family moved to Madame Verne's home town, Amiens in Picardy, to the northwest of Paris, where Jules Verne could pur-

sue his research in comfort (by 1895 he had accumu-
lated 20,000 filing cards), attend the Literary Academy, stroll, and sail. Work never ceased. Like Georges
Simenon, another tireless artisan of letters, the successful author used his successive boats as floating studies where much of his writing was done. He traveled.
He had always dreamed of discovering faraway lands.
Now he could afford even a voyage to America. But
most of his traveling, as before, was done on the
printed page.

In the generation before Verne's birth a great
Revolution, or rather a string of revolutions going off
like firecrackers, had introduced the politics of the impossible. In his own lifetime, a similar string of technological and scientific revolutions introduced the
impossible into everyday life. Mankind's experience
of space, time, speed, mass, movement, was radically
altered. It fell to Jules Verne to bring this home to millions of readers, explain it, illustrate it, and suggest
what it might mean for generations to come. Fascinated by the new world transformed by railroads and
great steamers, Verne stood at the crossroads of
present and future, a poet of technology, of science, of
the power and the menace that they hold. In 1869, he
imagined a mission to the moon that prefigured the
flight of *Apollo* 9 one century later. "Our space vehi-

cle," Frank Borman, the astronaut, wrote to Verne's grandson, "was launched from Florida, like [Verne's]; it had the same weight and the same height, and it splashed down in the Pacific a mere two and a half miles from the point mentioned in the novel." In 1879 he evoked the first artificial satellite; in 1882 he wrote about the sort of cosmic rays that physicists pursued between the two world wars.

The visionary writes about balloons, helicopters, heavier-than-air machines of every sort, about the earth (1864) and its geology, about lunar travel (1865, 1870), about polar exploration (1866), about underwater travel (1869), about electricity which powers the submarine *Nautilus* or produces a *téléphote* enabling people to see each other at a distance; and, of course, he writes about travel and exploration. All his stories are full of wonders, all a bit ominous, and few are more curious than the unpublished manuscript that Verne's great-grandson discovered in 1989, when the sale of a family home forced him to dispense with a great bronze safe long believed to be empty. The keys to the safe had been lost; it had to be opened with a blowtorch.

Temporarily tucked under a pile of linen, the pages discovered in 1989 were examined later, authenticated, and identified as a text that Hetzel had rejected late in 1863: "It's a hundred feet below *Five Weeks in a Balloon* . . . Your Michel is a real goose with his verses. Can't he carry parcels and remain a poet?" And the clincher: "No one today will believe your prophecy." Verne appears to have accepted Hetzel's verdict. Not so our generation. Published in 1994, *Paris in the Twentieth Century* proved an unexpected success, with two hundred thousand copies sold in its first year and thirty translations under way, including this one.

From the perspective of our century's end the future that Hetzel found unconvincing appears more plausible. The young stockbroker who hated the Stock Exchange warns against capitalism running riot, the young playwright whose plays had not quite made it warns against a society where culture is at low ebb. Michel is harnessed to his bank's Great Ledger as Orwell's Winston Smith is to the Disinformation Office; Michel's bookish uncle sounds like one of the Book People barely surviving in Ray Bradbury's *Fahrenheit 451.* And yet this arch-critic (and Radical city councillor of Amiens) is also an arch-conservative, especially in artistic tastes. To Berlioz, Verdi, Wagner, he prefers Gounod and Offenbach. Contemporary painting, for him, is nonexistent, Courbet is a gross peasant, painting lost its soul when it abandoned form (also the literary, poetic, thematic subjects of Romanticism). Let's not forget that 1863 was the year of the *Salon des refusés,* where Edouard Manet showed his *Déjeuner sur l'herbe:* bad vintage for a Romantic palate.

As for poetry, if T. S. Eliot could work in a bank, one doesn't see why poor Michel can't manage. His taste in poetry, at any rate, is odd even for mid-nineteenth century. When his friend admonishes "Your verses must celebrate the wonders of industry," Michel is firm: "Never." Yet industry's wonders and its commonplaces inspired Walt Whitman to sing snow shoes, rainproof coats, and the Brooklyn Bridge, "the latest dates, discoveries, inventions, societies, authors old and new . . ." Before too long, Carl Sandburg praised (ah, woe!) Chicago: "grocer of the world, maker of tools, champion of railroads, carrier of the nation's freight." What can one expect of Americans when even Parisiennes, Verne ruefully admits, are becoming Americanized? Yet everything can fuel the inspiration of an artist. The writings of Jules Verne are proof of this. Michel seems to ignore it.

Perhaps Verne's fascination with science was only secondhand. We know that at Amiens, where the university today bears his name, one of his own prize-giving speeches was devoted to a ringing denunciation of the bicycle; and that when, in 1894, Hetzel telephoned him at his club (his Amiens home lacked the newfangled contraption), Jules Verne, by now an elderly gentleman, took some time before he found which end of the receiver to put to his ear. He would be shocked to learn that in Chiapas, Mexico, the rebel Zapatista leader, Sub-Commandant Marcos, whom many French intellectuals admire, behaves like a high-tech Robin Hood connected to the Internet and accessible by dialing 3615 Zapata (*Le Monde,* June 29, 1996). Captain Nemo, take note.

Paris, 1996

Paris in the Twentieth Century

CHAPTER I

The Academic Credit Union

On August 13, 1960, a portion of the Parisian populace headed for the many Métro stations from which various local trains would take them to what had once been the Champ-de-Mars. It was Prize Day at the Academic Credit Union, the vast institution of public education, and over this solemn ceremony His Excellency the Minister of Improvements of the City of Paris was to preside.

The Academic Credit Union and the age's industrial aims were in perfect harmony: what the previous century called Progress had undergone enormous developments. Monopoly, that ne plus ultra of perfection, held the entire country within its talons; unions were founded, organized, the unexpected results of their proliferation would certainly have amazed our fathers.

Money had never been in short supply, though it was briefly frozen when the State nationalized the railroads; indeed there was an abundance of capital, and of capitalists as well, all seeking financial enterprises or industrial deals.

Hence, we shall not be surprised by what would have astonished a nineteenth-century Parisian and, among other wonders, by the creation of the Academic Credit Union, which had functioned successfully for over thirty years, under the financial leadership of Baron de Vercampin.

By dint of multiplying university branches, lycées, primary and secondary schools, Christian seminaries, cramming establishments, as well as the various asylums and orphanages, some sort of instruction had filtered down to the lowest layers of the social order. If no one read any longer, at least everyone could read, could even write. There was no ambitious artisan's son, no alienated farm boy, who failed to lay claim to an administrative position; the civil service developed in every possible way, shape, and form; we shall see, later on, what legions of employees the government controlled, and with what military precision.

For now, we need merely report how the means of education necessarily increased with the number of those to be educated. During the nineteenth century, had not construction firms, investment companies, and government-controlled corporations been devised when it became desirable to remake a new France, and a new Paris?

Now, construction and instruction are one and the same for businessmen, education being merely a somewhat less solid form of edification.

Such was the scheme, in 1937, of Baron de Vercampin, notorious for his far-flung financial dealings: it was his notion to establish a single vast institution, in which every branch of the tree of knowledge might flourish, it being the State's responsibility, moreover, to pollard, prune, and patrol such growth to the best of its ability.

The Baron merged the lycées of Paris and of the provinces, Sainte-Barbe and Rollin, as well as the various private institutions, into a single establishment, thereby centralizing the education of all France; investors responded to his appeal, for he presented the enterprise as an industrial operation. The Baron's skill was a guarantee in financial matters. Money flowed in. The Union was founded.

It was in 1937, during the reign of Napoleon V, that he had launched the enterprise; forty million copies of its prospectus were printed, on stationery that read:

ACADEMIC CREDIT UNION

Incorporated by law and testified to by Maître Mocquart
and Colleague, Notaries in Paris, on April 6, 1937, and ap-
proved by the Imperial Decree of May 19, 1937. Capital-
ized at one hundred million francs divided into one
hundred thousand shares of one thousand francs each

Board of Directors:

Baron de Vercampin, C., President
De Montaut, O., Manager of the Orleans Railroad
Vice Presidents
Garassu, Banker
Marquis d'Amphisbon, G.O., Senator
Roquamon, Colonel, Police Corps, G.C.
Dermangent, Deputy
Frappeloup, General Manager of the Academic Credit Union

The Union statutes followed, carefully expressed
in financial terms. As is apparent, no scholar's or professor's name appeared on the Board of Directors, a
matter of some reassurance with regard to the commercial prospects of the enterprise.

A Government Inspector supervised the Union's
operations and reported on them to the Minister of
Improvements of the City of Paris.

The Baron's notion was a good one, and singularly
practical, hence it succeeded above and beyond all ex-
pectations. In 1960, the Academic Union included no
fewer than 157,342 students, to whom knowledge was
imparted by mechanical means.

It must be confessed that the study of belles lettres and of ancient languages (including French) was
at this time virtually obsolete; Latin and Greek were
not only dead languages but buried as well; for form's
sake, some classes in literature were still taught,
though these were sparsely attended and inapprecia-
ble—indeed anything but appreciated. Dictionaries,
manuals, grammars, study guides and topic notes,
classical authors and the entire book trade in *de Viris,*
Quintus-Curtius, Sallust, and Livy peacefully crum-
bled to dust on the shelves of the old Hachette
publishing house; but introductions to mathematics,
textbooks on civil engineering, mechanics, physics,
chemistry, astronomy, courses in commerce, finance,
industrial arts—whatever concerned the market tendencies of the day—sold by the millions of copies.

In short, shares in the Union, which had multiplied
tenfold in twenty-two years, were now worth ten thousand francs apiece.

We shall insist no further upon the flourishing condition of the Academic Union; the figures, as an old
banking proverb has it, say it all.

Toward the end of the last century, the École Nor-
male was in evident decline; few among those young
people whose vocation inclined them toward a literary

career sought instruction here; the best among these had already discarded their academic gowns and flung themselves into the free-for-all of authorship and journalism; but even this distressing spectacle was no longer in evidence, for in the last ten years only scientific studies had posted candidates for the entrance examinations.

Yet if the last pedagogues of Greek and Latin were vanishing from their deserted classrooms, what splendid kudos, on the contrary, were awarded the science professors—and what eminence was theirs when it came to drawing a salary!

The sciences were now divided into six branches: under the main Division of Mathematics were ranged subdivisions of arithmetic, geometry, and algebra; there followed the main Divisions of Astronomy, Mechanics, Chemistry, and, most important of all, the Applied Sciences, with subdivisions of metallurgy, factory construction, mechanics, and chemistry adapted to the arts.

The living languages, except French, were in high favor; they were granted special consideration; in these disciplines an enthusiastic philologist might learn the two thousand languages and four thousand dialects spoken the world over. The Department of Chinese, for example, had included a great number of students ever since the colonization of Cochin China.

The Academic Credit Union possessed enormous buildings, constructed on the former Champs-de-Mars, now useless since there was no budgetary appropriation for martial undertakings. The site was a city in itself, a veritable metropolis with its different neighborhoods, its squares, streets, palaces, churches, and barracks, something like Nantes or Bordeaux, capable of accommodating one hundred and eighty thousand souls, including those of the professors and instructors.

A monumental arch opened onto the enormous main courtyard, known as the Study Field and surrounded by the Science Docks. Refectories, dormitories, the general study halls, where three thousand students could be accommodated, were well worth visiting, though they no longer astonished people accustomed, in the last fifty years, to similar wonders.

Hence the crowd eagerly made its way to this prize-giving ceremony, an invariably interesting observance which managed to attract, whether as friends, relatives, or merely observers, some five hundred thousand persons. The bulk of the crowd flowed in through the Grenelle station, then located at the end of the Rue de l'Université.

Yet despite the influx of this enormous public, everything proceeded in an orderly fashion; government employees, less zealous and consequently less intolerable than the agents of the old companies, deliberately left all the gates open; it had taken a hundred and fifty years to acknowledge this truth, that in dealing with crowds, it is wiser to multiply exits than to limit them.

The Study Field was sumptuously prepared for the Ceremony; but there is no space so great that it cannot eventually be filled, and the main courtyard soon reached its capacity.

At three o'clock the Minister of Improvements of the City of Paris made his formal entrance, accompanied by Baron de Vercampin and the members of the Board of Directors, the baron at His Excellency's right, Monsieur Frappeloup at his left; from the dais, a sea of heads as far as the eye could see. Then the various Establishment bands began playing their many selections, their tones and rhythms frequently unreconcilable. This obligatory cacophony seemed to have no ill effect upon the half million pairs of ears which absorbed it.

The Ceremony began. A murmurous silence fell—this was the moment of the speeches.

In the preceding century, a certain humorist by the name of Karr treated these prize-giving orations, more official jargon than actual Latin, as they deserved; at present, such subjects of derision would not have been available to him, for the old Latin bombast had fallen into desuetude. Who would have understood it? Not even the Deputy Director of Rhetoric!

A Chinese speech replaced it to great advantage; several passages provoked murmurs of approval; a bravura flourish on the comparative civilizations of the Sunda Islands was actually greeted with cries of *Bis!* This word was still understood.

Finally the Director of Applied Sciences stood up— a solemn moment: this was the principal item on the program.

His furious oration was remarkably similar to the whistles, groans, jangles, squeals, the thousand unpleasant noises which escape an active steam engine; the speaker's rapid delivery suggested a projectile hurtling at top speed; it would have been impossible to stem this high-pressure eloquence, and the grating phrases locked into one another like cogwheels.

To complete the illusion, the Director was sweating profusely, so that he was enveloped in a cloud of steam from head to foot.

"The Devil!" giggled his neighbor, an old man whose chiseled features expressed an immense disdain of such oratorical fatuity. "What do you make of that, Richelot?"

Monsieur Richelot was content to answer with a shrug.

"He's getting overheated," the old man went on, extending our metaphor. "Next you'll be telling me he has safety valves, but an exploding Director of Applied Sciences would set a nasty precedent!"

"Well put, Huguenin," replied Monsieur Richelot.

Vigorous cries for silence interrupted the two speakers, who exchanged a smile. Meanwhile the orator continued fast and furious, composing a veritable eulogy of the present, to the detriment of the past; he recited the litany of modern discoveries; he even let it be understood that in this regard the future would have little to contribute; he spoke with a benevolent scorn of the tiny Paris of 1860 and of the pygmy France of the nineteenth century; he enumerated with a copious supply of epithets such blessings of his age as the rapid communication between various points of the Capital, locomotives furrowing the asphalt of the boulevards, electric power in every home, carbonic acid now dethroning steam, and last of all the Ocean, the Ocean itself, whose waves now bathed the shores of Grenelle. He was sublime, lyrical, dithyrambic, in short quite intolerable and unjust, forgetting that the wonders of his century were already germinating in the projects of its predecessor.

Frenzied applause broke out at this same place where, one hundred and seventy years before, bravos had welcomed the Festival of Federation. Nonetheless, since everything—even speeches—must come to an end, the machine stopped. The oratorical exercises having been terminated without incident, the Ceremony proceeded to the actual awarding of the prizes.

The question given to the Grand Competition of Higher Mathematics was as follows: Given two circumferences OO′: from a point A on O, tangents are drawn to O′; the contact points of these tangents are joined: the tangent at A is drawn to the circumference O; what is the point of intersection of this tangent with the chord of contacts in the circumference O′?

The importance of such a theorem was universally understood. Many were familiar with how it had been solved according to a new method by the student Gigoujeu (François Némorin) from Briançon (Hautes Alpes). Bravos rang out when this name was called; it was uttered seventy-four times in the course of this memorable day: benches were broken in honor of the laureate, an activity which, even in 1960, was not yet merely a metaphor intended to describe the outbreaks of enthusiasm.

On this occasion Gigoujeu (François Némorin) was awarded a library of some three thousand volumes. The Academic Credit Union did things properly.

We cannot cite the endless nomenclature of the Sciences which were taught in this barracks of learning: an honors list of the day would have certainly astonished the great-grandfathers of these young scholars. The prize giving continued, and jeers rang out when some poor devil from the Division of Letters, shamed when his name was called, received a prize in Latin composition or an honorable mention for Greek translation. But there came a moment when the taunts redoubled, when sarcasm assumed its most disconcerting forms. This was when Monsieur Frappeloup pronounced the following words:

"First prize for Latin verse: Dufrénoy (Michel Jérome) from Vannes (Morbihan)." Hilarity was universal, amid remarks of this sort:

"A prize for Latin verse!"

"He must have been the only competitor!"

"Look at that darling of the Muses!"

"A habitué of Helicon!"

"A pillar of Parnassus!" et cetera, et cetera.

Nonetheless, Michel Jérome Dufrénoy stepped forward and faced down his detractors with a certain aplomb; he was a blond youth with a delightful countenance and a charming manner, neither awkward nor insolent. His long hair gave him a slightly girlish appearance, and his forehead shone as he advanced to the dais and snatched rather than received his prize from the Director's hand. This prize consisted of a single volume: the latest *Factory Manual.*

Michel glanced scornfully at the book and, flinging it to the ground, calmly returned to his seat, still wearing his crown and without even having kissed His Excellency's official cheeks.

"Well done," murmured Monsieur Richelot.

"Brave boy," said Monsieur Huguenin.

Murmurs broke out on all sides. Michel received them with a disdainful smile and sat down amid the catcalls of his schoolfellows.

This grand ceremony concluded without hindrance around seven in the evening; fifteen thousand prizes and twenty-seven thousand honorable mentions were distributed. The chief laureates of the Sciences dined that same evening at Baron de Vercampin's table, among members of the Administrative Council and the major stockholders.

The joy of these latter was explained by . . . figures! The dividend for the 1960 exercises had been set at 1,169 francs, 33 centimes per share. The current interest already exceeded the issue price.

CHAPTER II

A Panorama of the Streets of Paris

Michel Dufrénoy had followed the crowd, a mere drop of water in this stream transformed into a torrent by the removal of its obstructions. His excitement had subsided; the champion of Latin poetry became a timid young man amid this joyous throng; he felt alone, alien, and somehow isolated in the void. Where his fellow students hurried ahead, he made his way slowly, hesitantly, even more orphaned in this gathering of contented parents; he seemed to regret his labors, his school, his professor.

Without father or mother, he would now have to return to an unsympathetic household, certain of a grim reception for his Latin verse prize. "All right," he resolved, "let's get on with it! I shall endure their nastiness along with all the rest! My uncle is a literal-minded man, my aunt a practical woman, and my cousin a boy out for the main chance—ideas like mine are not welcome at home, but so what? Onward!"

Yet he proceeded quite unhurriedly, not being one of those schoolboys who rush into vacation like a subject people into freedom. His uncle and guardian had not even thought enough of the occasion to attend the prize giving; he knew what his nephew was "incapable" of, as he said, and would have been mortified to see him crowned a nursling of the Muses.

The crowd, however, impelled the wretched laureate forward; he felt himself borne on by the current like a drowning man. "A good comparison," he thought. "Here I am abandoned on the high seas; requiring the talents of a fish, all I have are the instincts of a bird; I want to live in space, in the ideal regions no longer visited—the land of dreams from which one never returns!"

Amid such reflections, jostled and buffeted, he reached the Grenelle station of the Métro. This line served the Left Bank of the river along the Boulevard Saint-Germain, which extended from the Gare d'Orléans to the buildings of the Academic Credit Union; here, curving toward the Seine, it crossed the river on the Pont d'Iéna, utilizing an upper level reserved for the railroad, and then joined the Right Bank line, which, through the Trocadéro tunnel, reached the Champs-Élysées and the axis of the Boulevards, which it followed to the Place de la Bastille, crossing the Pont d'Austerlitz to rejoin the Left Bank line.

This first ring of railroad tracks more or less encircled the ancient Paris of Louis XV, on the very site of the wall survived by this euphonious verse:

Le mur murant Paris rend Paris murmurant.

A second line reached the old faubourgs of Paris, extending for some thirty-two kilometers neighborhoods formerly located outside the peripheral boulevards. A third line followed the old orbital roadway for a length of some fifty-six kilometers. Finally, a fourth system connected the line of fortifications, its extent more than a hundred kilometers.

It is evident that Paris had burst its precincts of 1843 and made incursions into the Bois de Boulogne, the Plains of Issy, Vanves, Billancourt, Montrouge, Ivry, Saint-Mandé, Bagnolet, Pantin, Saint-Denis, Clichy, and Saint-Ouen. The heights of Meudon, Sèvres, and Saint-Cloud had blocked its development to the west. The delimitation of the present capital was marked by the forts of Mont Valérien, Saint-Denis, Aubervilliers, Romainville, Vincennes, Charenton, Vitry, Bicêtre, Montrouge, Vanves, and Issy; a city of one hundred and five kilometers in diameter, it had devoured the entire Department of the Seine.

Four concentric circles of railways thus formed the Metropolitan network; they were linked to one another by branch lines, which, on the Right Bank, extended the Boulevard de Magenta and the Boulevard Malesherbes and on the Left Bank, the Rué de Rennes and the Rue des Fossés-Saint-Victor. It was possible to circulate from one end of Paris to the other with the greatest speed.

These railways had existed since 1913; they had been built at State expense, following a system devised in the last century by the engineer Joanne. At that time, many projects were submitted to the Government, which had them examined by a council of civil engineers, those of the Ponts et Chausées no longer existing since 1889, when the École Polytechnique had been suppressed; but this council had long remained divided on the question; some members wanted to establish a surface line on the main streets of Paris; others recommended underground networks following London's example; but the first of these projects would have required the construction of barriers protecting the train tracks, whence an obvious encumbrance of pedestrians, carriages, carts, et cetera; the second involved enormous difficulties of execution; moreover, the prospect of even temporary burial in an endless tunnel was anything but attractive to the riders. Every roadway formerly created under these deplorable conditions had had to be remade, among others the Bois de Boulogne line, which by both bridges and tunnels compelled riders to interrupt reading their newspapers twenty-seven times during a trajectory of some twenty-three minutes.

Joanne's system seemed to unite all the virtues of rapidity, facility, and comfort, and indeed for the last fifty years the Metropolitan railways had functioned to universal satisfaction.

This system consisted of two separate roadbeds on which the trains proceeded in opposite directions; hence there was no possibility of a collision. Each of these tracks was established along the axis of the boulevards, five meters from the housefronts, above the outer rim of the sidewalks; elegant columns of galvanized bronze supported them and were attached to one another by cast armatures; at intervals these columns were attached to riverside houses, by means of transverse arcades. Thus, this long viaduct, supporting the railway track, formed a covered gallery, under which strollers found shelter from the elements; the asphalt roadway was reserved for carriages; by means of an elegant bridge the viaduct traversed the main

streets which crossed its path, and the railway, suspended at the height of the mezzanine floors, offered no obstacle to boulevard traffic.

Some riverside houses, transformed into waiting rooms, formed stations which communicated with the track by broad footbridges; underneath a double-ramp staircase gave access to the waiting room. Boulevard stations were located at the Trocadéro, the Madeleine, the Bonne Nouvelle department store, the Rue du Temple, and the Place de la Bastille.

This viaduct, supported on simple columns, would doubtless not have resisted the old means of traction, which required locomotives of enormous weight; but thanks to the application of new propulsors, the modern trains were quite light; they ran at intervals of ten minutes, each one bearing some thousand riders in its comfortably arranged cars.

The riverside houses suffered from neither steam nor smoke, quite simply because there was no locomotive: the trains ran by means of compressed air, according to the Williams System, recommended by the famous Belgian engineer Jobard, who flourished in the mid–nineteenth century.

A vector tube some twenty centimeters in diameter and two millimeters thick ran the entire length of the track between the two rails; it enclosed a soft-iron disc, which slid inside it under the action of several atmospheres of compressed air provided by the Catacomb Company of Paris. This disc, driven at high speed within the tube, like a bullet in its barrel, drew with it the first car of the train. But how was this car attached to the disc inside the tube, since this disc would have no communication with the exterior? By electromagnetic force.

In fact, the first car carried between its wheels magnets set on either side of the tube, as close as possible without actually touching it. These magnets operated through the walls of the tube on the soft-iron disc, which, sliding forward, drew the train after it, the compressed air being unable to escape through any outlet.*

When a train was to stop, a station employee opened a valve; air escaped and the disc remained motionless. As soon as the valve was closed, the air pushed on, and the train resumed its immediately rapid progress.

Thus by means of a system at once so simple and so easy to maintain—no smoke, no steam, no collision, and the passengers' freedom to ascend all the ramps—it seemed that these roadways must have existed since time immemorial.

* If an electromagnet can bear a weight of 1,000 kilograms on contact, its power of attraction is still that of 100 kilograms over a distance of five millimeters. (Author's note)

Young Dufrénoy bought his ticket at the Grenelle station and ten minutes later got off at the Madeleine; he walked down the steps to the boulevard and made for the Rue Impériale, which had been constructed on the axis of the Opéra down to the Gardens of the Tuileries. Crowds filled the streets; night was beginning to fall, and the luxury shops projected far out onto the sidewalks the brilliant patches of their electric light; streetlamps operated by the Way System—sending a positive electric charge through a thread of mercury—spread an incomparable radiance; they were connected by means of underground wires; at one and the same moment, the hundred thousand streetlamps of Paris came on. Nonetheless a few old-fashioned shops remained faithful to the old means of hydrocarburated gas; the exploitation of new coal pits permitted its current sale at ten centimes per cubic meter; but the Company made considerable profits, especially by distributing it as a mechanical agent.

In fact, of the countless carriages which clogged the boulevards, a great majority were horseless; they were invisibly powered by a motor which operated by gas combustion. This was the Lenoir machine applied to locomotion.

Invented in 1859, this machine had the initial advantage of doing away with boiler, firebox, and fuel; a little lighting gas, mixed with the air introduced under the piston and lit by an electric spark, produced the movement; gas hydrants, set up at the various carriage parking places, supplied the necessary hydrogen; new improvements had made it possible to get rid of the water formerly used to chill the machine's cylinder. The machine, then, was *simple and maneuverable;* up on his seat, the driver operated a steering wheel; a brake pedal, located under his foot, permitted an instant modification of the vehicle's speed.

The carriages, with the power of several horses, did not cost, per day, one eighth the price of a horse; the expense of the gas, carefully monitored, permitted calculation of the work done by each carriage, and the Company could no longer be deceived, as in the past, by its coachmen.

These gas cabs were responsible for a tremendous consumption of hydrogen, as were those enormous trucks loaded with stones and paving materials, which deployed some twenty to thirty horsepower. This Lenoir System had the further advantage of costing nothing when it was not in use, a saving impossible to realize with steam machines, which devour their fuel even when they are not in motion.

These swift means of transport operated in streets less clogged than in the past, for a ruling of the Ministry of Police forbade any cart, dray, or wagon to pass through the streets after ten in the morning, except for certain special routes.

These various improvements were certainly suited to this feverish century, during which the pressure of business permitted no rest and no delay.

What would one of our ancestors have said upon seeing these boulevards lit as brightly as by the sun, these thousand carriages circulating noiselessly on the silent asphalt of the streets, these stores as sumptuous as palaces, from which the light spread in brilliant patches, these avenues as broad as squares, these squares as wide as plains, these enormous hotels, which provided comfortable lodging for twenty thousand travelers, these wonderfully light viaducts, these long, elegant galleries, these bridges flung from street to street, and finally these glittering trains, which seemed to furrow the air with fantastic speed?

No doubt he would have been astonished; but the men of 1960 were no longer lost in admiration of such marvels; they exploited them quite calmly, without being any the happier, for, from their hurried gait, their peremptory manner, their American "dash," it was apparent that the demon of wealth impelled them onward without mercy or relief.

CHAPTER III

An Eminently Practical Family

At length the young man reached the house of his uncle, Monsieur Stanislas Boutardin, banker and director of the Catacomb Company of Paris.

It was in a magnificent mansion on the Rue Impériale that this important person resided, an enormous structure in wonderfully bad taste, sporting a multitude of plate-glass windows, a veritable barracks transformed into a private residence, not so much imposing as ponderous. The ground floor and outbuildings were occupied by offices.

"So this is where the rest of my life is going to be spent," Michel mused as he walked in. "Must I abandon all hope at the door?" And he was overcome by an almost invincible longing to run away, but managed to control himself; he pressed the electric button of the carriage entrance, and the doors, operated by a hidden spring, noiselessly opened and closed behind him.

A huge courtyard led to the offices, arranged in a circle under a ground-glass ceiling; at the rear was a large garage, where several gas cabs awaited the master's orders.

Michel made for the elevator, a narrow chamber with a narrow tufted banquette around the walls; a servant in orange livery was on duty day and night. "Monsieur Boutardin," Michel announced.

"Monsieur Boutardin has just begun his dinner," replied the footman.

"Be so good as to tell him his nephew, Monsieur Dufrénoy, is here."

The footman touched a metal button set into the woodwork, and the elevator rose imperceptibly to the first floor, where the dining room was located. The servant announced Michel Dufrénoy.

Monsieur Boutardin, Madame Boutardin, and their son were seated around the table and met the young man's appearance with a profound silence; his place was set for him, the meal had just begun; at a sign from his uncle, Michel joined the banquet. No one spoke a word to him. Apparently his disaster was known to all. He could not eat a mouthful.

There was a funereal air about this meal; the servants performed their tasks in perfect silence; the various dishes ascended noiselessly in chutes set in the walls; they were opulent with a touch of avarice, and seemed to nourish the diners with a certain reluctance, a certain regret. In this absurdly gilded, mournful room, everyone chewed rapidly and without conviction. The point, of course, was not to be fed but to have earned the material on which to feed. Michel perceived the nuance, and choked on it. At dessert, his uncle spoke for the first time: "Tomorrow, sir, first thing in the morning, I should like a word with you." Michel bowed without speaking; an orange-liveried servant led him to his room; the young man went to bed; the hexagonal ceiling reminded him of a host of geometrical theorems; he dreamed, in spite of himself, of right-angle triangles whose hypotenuse had been . . . reduced. "What a family!" he murmured to himself in the depths of his troubled sleep.

Monsieur Stanislas Boutardin was the natural product of this age of industrial development; he had sprouted in a greenhouse, rather than among the elements; a practical man in every particular, he did nothing which was not of some utilitarian function, orienting his merest ideas to use, with an excessive craving to be useful, which turned into a truly ideal egotism, joining the useful to the disagreeable, as Horace might have said; his vanity was apparent in his words and even more in his gestures, and he would not have allowed his shadow to precede him; he expressed himself in grams and centimeters, and at all times carried a cane marked off in metrical divisions, which afforded him a wide knowledge of the things of this world; he utterly scorned the arts, and artists even more, though he was quite prepared to suggest that he knew such creatures; for him, painting stopped with a tinted drawing, and drawing with a diagram, sculpture with a plaster cast, music with the whistle of locomotives, and literature with stock market quotations.

This man, raised in mechanics, accounted for life by gears and transmissions; he moved quite regularly, with the least possible friction, like a piston in a perfectly reamed cylinder; he transmitted his uniform movements to his wife, to his son, to his employees and his servants, all veritable tool machines, from which he, the motor force, derived the maximum possible profit.

A base nature, in short, incapable of a good impulse, or, for that matter, of a bad one; he was neither wicked nor good, insignificant, often ill lubricated, noisy, horribly vulgar.

He had made an enormous fortune, if such activity can be called making. The industrial impulse of the century impelled him; hence he showed a certain gratitude toward industry, which he worshiped as a goddess; he was the first to adopt, for his household, the spun-metal garments which first appeared around

1934. Such textiles, moreover, were as soft to the touch as cashmere, though scarcely of much warmth; but in winter, with a good lining, they sufficed; and when such everlasting garments happened to rust, they were simply filed down and repainted in the colors of the moment.

The banker's social position was as follows: Director of the Catacomb Company of Paris and of the Driving Force in the Home.

The enterprises of this company consisted in warehousing the air in those huge underground vaults so long unused; here it was stored under a pressure of forty to fifty atmospheres, a constant force which conduits led to the factories and mills, wherever a mechanical action became necessary. This compressed air served, as we have seen, to power the trains on the elevated railways of the boulevards. Eighteen hundred fifty-three windmills, constructed on the Plain of Montrouge, compressed the air by means of pumps within these enormous reservoirs.

This conception, certainly a highly practical one which came down to the employment of natural forces, was readily anticipated by the banker Boutardin; he became the Director of this important company while remaining a member of fifteen or twenty supervisory boards, vice president of the Society of Tow Locomotives, administrative director of the Amalgamated Asphalt Agencies, et cetera, et cetera.

Some forty years ago he had married Mademoiselle Athénaïs Dufrénoy, Michel's aunt; she was certainly the worthy and cantankerous companion of a banker—homely, stout, having all the qualities of a bookkeeper and a cashier, nothing of a woman; she was expert in double entry, and would had invented a triple version if need be; a true administratrix, the female of any and every administrator.

Did she love Monsieur Boutardin, and was she loved by him in return? Yes, insofar as these businesslike hearts could love; a comparison will complete the portrait of the pair: she was the locomotive and he the engineer; he kept her in good condition, oiled and polished her, and thus she had rolled forward for a good half century, with about as much sense and imagination as a Crampton Motor.

Unnecessary to add that she never derailed.

As for their son, multiply his mother by his father, and you have Athanase Boutardin for a coefficient, chief associate of the banking house Casmodage and Co., an agreeable boy who took after his father for high spirits, and after his mother for elegance. It was impossible to pass a witty remark in his presence; it seemed to miss him altogether, and his brows frowned over his vacant eyes. He had won the first banking prize in the grand competition. It might be said that he not only made money work but wore it out; he smelled of usury; he was planning to marry some dreadful creature whose dowry would energetically make up for her ugliness. At twenty, he already wore aluminum-framed spectacles. His narrow and deep-rutted mind impelled him to tease his clerks by touches of the whip. One of his tricks consisted of claiming his cashbox was empty, whereas it was stuffed with gold and notes. He was a wretched creature, without youth, without heart, without friends. Greatly admired by his father.

Such was this family, this domestic trinity from which young Dufrénoy was seeking aid and protection. Monsieur Dufrénoy, Madame Boutardin's brother, had possessed all the sentimental delicacy and the sensitivity which in his sister were translated as asperities. This poor artist, a highly talented musician, born for a better age, succumbed in youth to his labors, bequeathing his son no more than his poetical tendencies, his aptitudes, and his aspirations.

Michel knew he had an uncle somewhere, a certain Huguenin, whose name was never mentioned, one of those learned, modest, poor, resigned creatures who are the shame of opulent families. But Michel was forbidden to see him, and he had never even encountered him; hence there was no hope in that direction.

The orphan's situation in the world was, therefore, nicely determined: on the one hand, an uncle incapable of coming to his aid, on the other, a family rich in those qualities which are readily coined, with just enough heart to send the blood through its arteries.

There was not much here for which to thank Providence.

The next day, Michel went downstairs to his uncle's office, a somber chamber if ever there was one, and papered with a serious material: here were gathered the banker, his wife, and his son. The occasion threatened to be a solemn one.

Monsieur Boutardin, standing on the hearth, one hand in his vest and puffing out his chest, expressed himself in the following terms:

"Monsieur, you are about to hear certain words which I must ask you to engrave upon your memory. Your father was an artist—a word which says it all. I should like to think that you have not inherited his unfortunate instincts. Yet I have discerned in you certain seeds which must be rooted out. You tend to flounder in the sands of the ideal, and hitherto the clearest result of your efforts has been this prize for Latin verses, which you so shamefully brought here yesterday. Let us reckon up the situation. You are without fortune, which is a blunder. Moreover, you have no parents. Now, I want no poets in my family, you must realize. I want none of those individuals who spit their rhymes in people's faces; you have a wealthy family—do not compromise us. Now, the artist is not far from the grimacing humbug to whom I toss a hundred sous from my box for him to entertain my digestion. You understand me. No talent. Capacities. Since I have observed no particular aptitude in you, I have decided that you must enter the Casmodage and Co. banking house, under the direction of your cousin; take him as your example. Work to become a practical man! Remember that a certain share of the blood of the Boutardins flows in your veins, and the better to recall my words, take heed never to forget them."

In 1960, as may be seen, the race of Prudhomme was not yet extinct; the finest traditions had been preserved. What could Michel reply to such a diatribe? Nothing, hence he was silent, while his aunt and his cousin nodded their approval.

"Your vacation," the banker resumed, "begins this morning, and ends this evening. Tomorrow you shall be introduced to the head of Casmodage and Co. You may go."

The young man left his uncle's office, eyes filled with tears; yet he braced himself against despair. "I have no more than a single day of freedom," he mused, "at least I shall spend it as I please; I have a little money, and *it* I shall spend on books beginning with the great poets and illustrious authors of the last century. Each evening they will console me for the vexations of each day."

CHAPTER IV

Concerning Some Nineteenth-Century Authors, and the Difficulty of Obtaining Them

Michel hurried out into the street and made for the Five Quarters Bookstore, an enormous warehouse on the Rue de la Paix, run by an important State official. "All the productions of the human mind must be here," the young man reflected, as he entered a huge vestibule, in the center of which a telegraph bureau kept in touch with the remotest branch stores. A legion of employees kept rushing past, and counterweighted lifts, set into the walls, were raising the clerks to the upper shelves of the various rooms; there was a considerable crowd in front of the telegraph desk, and porters were struggling under their loads of books.

Amazed, Michel vainly attempted to estimate the number of books that covered the walls from floor to ceiling, their rows vanishing among the endless galleries of this imperial establishment. "I'll never manage to read all this," he thought, taking his place in line; at last he reached the window.

"What is it you want, sir?" he was asked by the clerk in charge of requests.

"I'd like the complete works of Victor Hugo," Michel replied.

The clerk's eyes widened. "Victor Hugo? What's he written?"

"He's one of the great poets of the nineteenth century, actually the greatest," the young man answered, blushing as he spoke.

"Do you know anything about this?" the man at the desk asked a second clerk in charge of research.

"Never heard of him," came the answer. "You're sure that's the name?"

"Absolutely sure."

"The thing is," the clerk continued, "we rarely sell literary works here. But if you're sure of the name . . . Rhugo, Rhugo . . ." he murmured, tapping out the name.

"Hugo," Michel repeated. "And while you're at it, please ask for Balzac, Musset, Lamartine . . ."

"Scholars?"

"No! They're authors."

"Living?"

"They've been dead for over a century."

"Sir, we'll do all we can to help you, but I'm afraid our efforts will require some time, and even then I'm not sure . . ."

"I'll wait," Michel replied. And he stepped out of line into a corner, abashed. So all that fame had lasted less than a hundred years! *Les Orientales, Les Méditations, La Comédie Humaine*—forgotten, lost, unknown! Yet here were huge crates of books which giant steam cranes were unloading in the courtyards, and buyers were crowding around the purchase desk. But one of them was asking for *Stress Theory* in twenty volumes, another for an *Abstract of Electric Problems,* this one for *A Practical Treatise for the Lubrication of Driveshafts,* and that one for the latest *Monograph on Cancer of the Brain.*

"How strange!" mused Michel. "All of science and industry here, just as at school, and nothing for art! I must sound like a madman, asking for literary works here—am I insane?" Michel lost himself in such reflections for a good hour; the searches continued, the telegraph operated uninterruptedly, and the names of "his" authors were confirmed; cellars and attics were ransacked, but in vain. He would have to give up.

"Monsieur," a clerk in charge of the Response Desk informed him, "we don't have any of this. No doubt these authors were obscure in their own period, and their works haven't been reprinted . . ."

"There must have been at least half a million copies of *Notre-Dame de Paris* published in Hugo's lifetime," Michel replied.

"I believe you, sir, but the only old author reprinted nowadays is Paul de Kock, a moralist of the last century; it seems to be very nicely written, and if you'd like—"

"I'll look elsewhere," Michel answered.

"Oh, you can comb the entire city. What you can't find here won't turn up anywhere else, I can promise you that!"

"We'll see," Michel said as he walked away.

"But, sir," the clerk persisted, worthy in his zeal of being a wine salesman, "might you be interested in any works of contemporary literature? We have some items here that have enjoyed a certain success in recent years—they haven't sold badly for poetry . . ."

"Ah!" said Michel, tempted, "you have modern poems?"

"Of course. For instance, Martillac's *Electric Harmonies,* which won a prize last year from the Academy of Sciences, and Monsieur de Pulfasse's *Meditations on Oxygen;* and we have the *Poetic Parallelogram,* and even the *Decarbonated Odes . . .*"

Michel couldn't bear hearing another word and found himself outside again, stupefied and overcome.

Not even this tiny amount of art had escaped the pernicious influence of the age! Science, Chemistry, Mechanics had invaded the realm of poetry! "And such
things are read," he murmured as he hurried through
the streets, "perhaps even bought! And signed by the
authors and placed on the shelves marked *Literature*.
But not one copy of Balzac, not one work by Victor
Hugo! Where can I find such things—where, if not the
Library . . ."

Almost running now, Michel made his way to the
Imperial Library; its buildings, amazingly enlarged,
now extended along a great part of the Rue de Riche-
lieu from the Rue Neuve-des-Petits-Champs to the Rue
de la Bourse. The books, constantly accumulating, had
burst through the walls of the old Hôtel de Nevers.
Each year fabulous quantities of scientific works were
printed; there were not suppliers enough for the de-
mand, and the State itself had turned publisher: the
nine hundred volumes bequeathed by Charles V, multiplied a thousand times, would not have equaled the
number now registered in the library; the eight hundred thousand volumes possessed in 1860 now reached
over two million.

Michel asked for the section of the buildings
reserved for literature and followed the stairway
through Hieroglyphics, which some workmen were

restoring with shovels and pickaxes. Having reached the Hall of Letters, Michel found it deserted, and stranger today in its abandonment than when it had formerly been filled with studious throngs. A few foreigners still visited the place as if it were the Sahara, and were shown where an Arab died in 1875, at the same table he had occupied all his life.

The formalities necessary to obtain a work were quite complicated; the borrower's form had to contain the book's title, format, publication date, edition number, and the author's name—in other words, unless one was already informed, one could not become so. At the bottom, spaces were left to indicate the borrower's age, address, profession, and purpose of research.

Michel obeyed these regulations and handed his properly filled-out form to the librarian sleeping at his desk; following his example, the pages were snoring loudly on chairs set around the wall; their functions had become a sinecure as complete as those of the ushers at the Comédie-Française. The librarian, waking with a start, stared at the bold young man; he read the form and appeared to be stupefied at the request; after much deliberation, to Michel's alarm, he sent the latter to a subordinate official working near his own window, but at a separate little desk. Michel found himself facing a man of about seventy, bright-eyed and smiling, with the look of a scholar who believed he knew nothing. This modest clerk took Michel's form and read it attentively. "You want the authors of the nineteenth century," he said. "That's quite an honor for them—it will allow us to dust them off. As we say here, Monsieur . . . Michel Dufrénoy?" At this name, the old man's head jerked up. "You are Michel Dufrénoy?" he exclaimed. "Of course you are, I hadn't really taken a look at you!"

"You know me?"

"Do I know you!" The old man could not go on; overpowering emotion was evident on his kindly countenance; he held out his hand, and Michel, trustingly, shook it with great affection. "I am your uncle," the librarian finally stammered out, "your old Uncle Huguenin, your poor mother's brother."

"*You* are my uncle!" Michel exclaimed, deeply moved.

"You don't know me, but I know you, my boy. I was there when you won your splendid prize for Latin Versification! My heart was pounding, and you never knew a thing about it."

"Uncle!"

"It's not your fault, dear fellow, I know. I was standing in back, far away from you, so as not to get you into trouble with your aunt's family; but I have been following your studies step by step, day by day! I used to tell myself: it's not possible that my sister's boy, the son of that great artist, has preserved none of those poetic instincts that so distinguished his father; nor was I mistaken, since here you are, asking me for our great French poets! Yes, my boy! I shall give them to you, we shall read them together! No one will trouble us here! No one bothers to keep an eye on us! Let me embrace you for the first time!"

The old man clasped his nephew in his arms, and the boy felt himself restored to life in that embrace. It was the sweetest emotion of his life up to that very moment. "But, Uncle," he asked, "how have you found out what was happening to me all during my childhood?"

"Dear boy, I have a friend who is very fond of you, your old Professor Richelot, and through him I learned that you were one of us! I saw you at work; I read the theme you wrote in Latin verse—a difficult subject to handle, certainly, because of the proper names: *Marshal Pélissier on the Malacoff Tower*. But that's how it goes, they're always about old historical subjects, and, my word, you managed it very nicely!"

"Not really!"

"Oh yes," the old scholar continued, "you made two strong beats and two weak ones for Pelissierus, one strong and two weaks for Malacoff, and you were right: you know, I still remember those two fine lines:

Iam Pelissiero pendenti ex turre Malacoff
Sebastopolitam concedit Jupiter urbem . . .

Ah, my boy, how many times, had it not been for that family who despise me and who, after all, were paying for your education—how many times I would have encouraged your splendid inspirations! But now, you will visit me here, and often!"

"Every evening, Uncle, when I am free to do so."

"But isn't this your vacation?"

"Vacation! Tomorrow morning, Uncle, I must start working in my cousin's bank."

"You in a bank, my boy!" exclaimed the old man. "You in business! Lord, what will become of you? A poor old wretch like me is no use to you, that's for sure, but my dear fellow, with your ideas, and your talents, you were born too late, I dare not say too soon, for the way things are going, we daren't even hope for the future!"

"But can't I refuse? Am I not a free agent?"

"No, you're not. Monsieur Boutardin is unfortunately more than your uncle—he is your guardian; I can't—I mustn't encourage you to follow a deadly path;

no, you're still young; work for your independence, and then, if your tastes have not altered and I am still in this world, come to see me."

"But the banking profession disgusts me!" Michel exclaimed.

"I'm sure it does, my boy, and if there were room for two of us in my place, I'd say to you: come and live with me, we'll be happy together; but such an existence would lead nowhere, and it's absolutely necessary that you be led somewhere. . . . No! Work, my boy! forget me for a few years; I'd only give you bad advice; don't mention our meeting to your uncle—it might do you harm; don't think about an old man who would be dead long since, were it not for his dear habit of coming here every day and finding his old friends on these shelves."

"When I'm free . . . ," said Michel.

"Yes! in two years! You're sixteen now, you'll be on your own at eighteen, we can wait; but don't forget, Michel, that I shall always have a warm welcome for you, a piece of good advice, and a loving heart. Come and see me!" added the old man, contradicting his own counsels.

"Yes, Uncle, I will. Where do you live?"

"Oh, a long way away, out on the Saint-Denis Plain, but the Boulevard Malesherbes Line takes me very close—I have a chilly little room out there, but it will be big enough when you come to see me, and warm enough when I hold your hands in mine."

The conversation between uncle and nephew continued in this fashion; the old scholar sought to smother just those tendencies he most admired in the young man, and his words constantly betrayed his intention; an artist's situation, as he well knew, was hopeless, déclassé, impossible. They went on talking of everything under the sun. The old man offered himself like an old book which his nephew might come and leaf through from time to time, good at best for telling him about the good old days. Michel mentioned his reason for visiting the library and questioned his uncle about the decadence of literature.

"Literature is dead, my boy," the uncle replied. "Look at these empty rooms, and these books buried in their dust; no one reads anymore; I am the guardian of a cemetery here, and exhumation is forbidden."

During this conversation time passed without their noticing it. "Four o'clock!" exclaimed the uncle. "I'm afraid I must leave you."

"I'll see you soon," Michel promised.

"Yes! No! My boy, never speak of literature, never speak of art! Accept the situation as it is! You are Monsieur Boutardin's ward before being your Uncle Huguenin's nephew!"

"Let me walk you some of the way," said young Dufrénoy.

"No, someone might see us. I'll go by myself."

"Then till next Sunday, Uncle."

"Till Sunday, my dear boy."

Michel left first, but waited in the street; he saw the old man heading toward the boulevard, his steps still confident; he followed him, at a distance, all the way to the Madeleine station. "At last," he rejoiced, "I'm no longer alone in the world!"

He returned to his uncle's mansion. Luckily the Boutardins were dining in town, and it was alone in his peaceful little room that Michel spent his first and last vacation evening.

CHAPTER V

Which Treats of Calculating Machines and Self-protecting Safes

At eight o'clock the next morning, Michel Dufrénoy headed for the offices of the Casmodage and Co. Bank, which occupied, in the Rue Neuve-Drouot, one of those buildings erected on the site of the old Opéra; the young man was taken into a vast parallelogram filled with strangely shaped machines. At first he could not make out what they were: they looked rather like huge pianos.

Glancing toward the adjacent office, Michel caught sight of several enormous safes: not only did these resemble fortresses but they were even crenellated, and each of them could easily have lodged a garrison of twenty men.

Michel could not help shuddering at the sight of these armored coffers. "They look absolutely bombproof," he reflected.

A middle-aged man, his morning quill already behind his ear, was solemnly strolling among these monuments. Michel soon identified him as belonging to the genus *Number,* order *Cashier;* precise, orderly, and ill-tempered, this individual invariably accepted money with enthusiasm and paid it out only grudgingly. He seemed to regard such disbursements as thefts; receipts, on the other hand, he treated as restitutions. Some sixty clerks, copyists, and shipping agents were busily scribbling and calculating under his direction. Michel was to take his place among them; an office boy led him to the important personage who was expecting him. "Monsieur," the Cashier remarked, "when you enter these precincts, you will first of all forget that you belong to the Boutardin family. That is the procedure."

"It suits me fine," Michel replied.

"To begin your apprenticeship, you will be assigned to Machine Number Four." Michel turned around and discovered the calculating machine behind him. It had been several centuries since Pascal had constructed a device of this kind, whose conception had seemed so remarkable at the time. Since then, the architect Perrault, Count Stanhope, Thomas de Colmar, Mauret and Jayet had made any number of valuable modifications to such machines. The Casmodage Bank possessed veritable masterpieces of the genre, instruments which indeed did resemble huge pianos: by operating a sort of keyboard, sums were instantaneously produced, remainders, products, quotients, rules of proportion, calculations of amortization and of interest compounded for infinite periods and at all possible rates. There were high notes which afforded up to one hundred fifty percent! The capacities of these extraordinary machines would easily have defeated even the Mondeux and the [proper name missing in the manuscript].

Except that you had to know how to play them: Michel would be obliged to take lessons in fingering. It was evident that he had entered the employment of a banking house which required and adopted all the resources of technology. Moreover, at this period, the volume of business and the diversity of correspondence gave mere office devices an extraordinary importance. For example, the Casmodage Bank issued no less than three thousand letters a day, posted to every corner of the world. A fifteen-horsepower Lenoir never ceased copying these letters, which five hundred employees incessantly fed into it.

Nevertheless electric telegraphy must have greatly diminished the number of letters, for new improvements now permitted the sender to correspond directly with the addressee; secrecy of correspondence was thus preserved, and the most intricate deals could be transacted over great distances. Each banking house had its own special wires, according to the Wheatstone System long since in use throughout England. Quotations of countless stocks on the international market were automatically inscribed on dials utilized by the Exchanges of Paris, London, Frankfurt, Amsterdam, Turin, Berlin, Vienna, Saint Petersburg, Constantinople, New York, Valparaiso, Calcutta, Sydney, Peking, and Nuku Hiva. Further, photographic telegraphy, invented during the last century by Professor Giovanni Caselli of Florence, permitted transmission of the facsimile of any form of writing or illustration, whether manuscript or print, and letters of credit or contracts could now be signed at a distance of five thousand leagues.

The telegraph network now covered the entire surface of the earth's continents and the depths of the seas; America was not more than a second away from Europe, and in a formal experiment made in London in 1903, two agents corresponded with each other after having caused their dispatches to circumnavigate the globe.

It is apparent that in this phase of business, the consumption of paper had increased to unheard-of proportions; France, which a century before had produced some sixty million kilograms of paper, now utilized more than three hundred million kilograms;

moreover there was no longer any need to fear the exhaustion of rag-based stocks, which had been advantageously replaced by alfa, aloes, Jerusalem artichoke, lupine, and twenty other cheaply cultivated plants; in twelve hours, the Watt and Burgess processes could turn a piece of wood into a splendid grade of paper; forests no longer served for firewood, but for printing.

The Casmodage Bank had been one of the first to adopt this wood-based paper; when used for contracts, letters, and deeds, it was prepared with Lemfelder's gallic acid, which rendered it impregnable to the chemical agents of forgers; since the number of thieves had increased with the volume of commerce, it was essential to take protective measures.

Such was this establishment, in which enormous deals were transacted. Young Dufrénoy was to play the most modest of roles in it, as the first servant of his calculating machine, and would enter upon his functions that very day. Such mechanical labor was very difficult for him, for he did not possess the sacred fire, and the machine functioned quite poorly under his fingers; try as he would, a month after his installation, he made more errors than on his first day, and yet he struggled with the infernal keyboard until he felt he had reached the brink of madness.

He was kept under severe discipline, moreover, in order to break any impulses of independence or artistic instincts; he had no Sunday free, and no evening to spend with his uncle, and his only consolation was to write him, in secret. Soon discouragement and disgust got the better of him, and he grew incapable of continuing the tasks he had been assigned. At the end of November, the following conversation regarding him occurred between Monsieur Casmodage, Boutardin fils, and the Cashier:

"The boy is monumentally inept," the banker observed.

"The claims of truth oblige me to agree," replied the Cashier.

"He is what used to be called an artist," Athanase broke in, "and what we would call a ninny."

"In his hands, the machine is becoming a dangerous instrument," returned the banker. "He brings us sums instead of subtractions, and he's never been able to give us a calculation of interest at only fifteen percent!"

"A pathetic case," observed the cousin.

"But how can we use him?" inquired the Cashier.

"Can he read?" asked Monsieur Casmodage.

"Presumably," Athanase replied.

"We might use him for the Ledger; he could dictate to Quinsonnas, who's been asking for an assistant."

"A fine idea," observed the cousin. "He's not good for much else besides dictating—his handwriting is dreadful."

"And nowadays everyone writes such a fine hand," commented the Cashier.

"If he doesn't work out at this new job," declared Monsieur Casmodage, "he won't be good for anything but sweeping the offices!"

"And even that . . . ," observed the cousin.

"Bring him in," said the banker.

Michel appeared before the redoubtable triumvirate. "Monsieur Dufrénoy," said the Director, his lips spread in the most scornful of smiles, "your notorious incapacity compels us to withdraw you from the operation of Machine Number Four; the results you have been producing are a constant cause of errors in our statements; this cannot continue."

"I regret the fact, Monsieur—" Michel replied coldly.

"Your regrets are of no use whatever," the banker replied severely; "henceforth you will be assigned to the Ledger. I am told that you can read. You will dictate."

Michel said nothing. The change meant nothing to him; the Ledger and the Machine were interchangeable as far as he was concerned. He then withdrew, after asking when his position would change.

"Tomorrow," answered Athanase. "Monsieur Quinsonnas will be informed."

The young man left the offices, thinking not of his new employment but of this Quinsonnas, whose very name alarmed him! What could such a man be? Some individual who had grown old copying articles for the Ledger, balancing accounts current for sixty years, subject to the fever of outstanding balances and the frenzy of double entry! Michel marveled that the bookkeeper had not yet been replaced by a machine.

Yet he felt an authentic joy at abandoning his calculating machine; he was proud of having operated it so poorly; its pseudopiano aspect had repulsed him. Back in his room, he soon found night coming on amid his reflections; he went to bed but could not sleep; a sort of nightmare overwhelmed his brain. The Ledger flashed before him, assuming fantastic dimensions; sometimes he felt he was being pressed between the white pages like some dried plant in an herbal, or else caught in the binding, which squeezed him in its brazen clamps. He got up in great agitation, seized by an invincible desire to examine this formidable device.

"It's all nonsense," he told himself, "but at least I'll get to the bottom of it." He leaped out of bed, opened the door of his room, and groping, stumbling, arms extended, eyes blinking, ventured downstairs into the offices.

The huge halls were dark and silent, where only a few hours ago the din of finance—the clink of coins, the rustle of banknotes, the squeak of pens on paper—had filled them with that sound so peculiar to banking houses. Michel groped his way ahead, losing himself in the center of this labyrinth; he was not too certain where the Ledger was situated but felt sure to find it; first he would have to cross the hall of the machines—he recognized them in the darkness. "They're sleeping," he mused, "not calculating now." And he continued his reconnaissance, passing through the hall of the giant safes, bumping into one at every step. Suddenly he felt the ground give way under his feet, a dreadful noise filled his ears; all the doors slammed shut; the bolts and locks slid into place, and deafening whistles were set off up in the cornices; a sudden illumination filled the offices with garish light, while Michel seemed to be sliding into some bottomless abyss.

Dazed and terrified, the moment the ground seemed to be solid under his feet, he tried to run away. Impossible! He was a prisoner now, caught in an iron cage.

At that very moment, several men in various stages of undress rushed toward him.

"A thief!" exclaimed one.

"We've got him!" said another.

"Go call the police!"

Michel instantly recognized among these witnesses of his disaster Monsieur Casmodage and Cousin Athanase.

"You!" exclaimed the former.

"Him!" exclaimed the latter.

"You were trying to crack my safe!"

"That's the last straw!"

"He's a sleepwalker," someone said.

For the honor of young Dufrénoy, this notion rallied the majority of these men in their nightshirts. The prisoner was uncaged, innocent victim of these ultramodern safes, which protected themselves automatically. Stretching out his arms in the dark, Michel had brushed against the Bond Safe, an apparatus of virginal sensitivity; an alarm had immediately sounded and the floor opened by means of a sliding panel, while the electric lights were automatically turned on at the sound of the locking doors. The employees, wakened by powerful buzzers, rushed toward the cage which had been lowered into the cellar.

"That will teach you," the banker scolded the young man, "to wander around where you have no business being!"

Shamed, Michel found nothing to say in his defense.

"Clever, that machine!" exclaimed Athanase.

"Still," interjected Monsieur Casmodage, "it won't be complete until the thief is deposited in a police wagon and automatically driven to the Prefecture!"

"As a matter of fact," Michel thought, "not until the machine itself applies the article of the criminal code relative to trespass and burglary!" But he kept this refinement to himself, and fled to his room amid loud bursts of laughter.

CHAPTER VI

In Which Quinsonnas Appears
on the Ledger's Summit

The next day, Michel made his way to the bookkeeping offices amid ironic whispers; his adventure of the night before had run from mouth to mouth, and this morning not one clerk troubled to suppress his laughter.

Michel arrived in a vast hall under a ground-glass dome; in the center, on a single pedestal, a marvel of mechanical contrivance, towered the Ledger of the Casmodage Bank. It deserved its capital letter, for it was some six meters high; an intricate mechanism allowed it to be aimed like a telescope at every point on the horizon; a system of delicate catwalks, ingeniously combined, could be raised or lowered according to the writer's needs.

On white pages some 3 meters wide, the bank's daily operations were spelled out in letters 8 centimeters high. *Petty Cash, General Cash, Loans,* silhouetted in gold ink, delighted the attention of those who had a taste for such things. Other many-colored inks enlivened the amounts carried forward and the pagination; as for the figures, splendidly superimposed in the addition columns, francs were expressed in scarlet, and centimes, carried to the third decimal, glowed a dark green.

Michel was astounded at the sight of this monument. He asked for Monsieur Quinsonnas and was shown a young man perched on the highest catwalk; mounting a spiral staircase, he reached the Ledger's summit in a very few moments. Here he found Monsieur Quinsonnas was illuminating a capital *F* one meter high with incomparable dexterity.

"Monsieur Quinsonnas?"

"Be so good as to come closer," replied the bookkeeper. "To whom have I the honor of speaking?"

"To . . . to Monsieur Dufrénoy."

"Would you be the hero of last night's adventure which—"

"I am," Michel answered bravely.

"It does you credit," Quinsonnas continued. "You are an honest man—a thief would never have let himself be caught. Such is my opinion."

Michel stared hard at his interlocutor—was he being teased? The bookkeeper's tremendously serious countenance permitted no such supposition. "I await your orders," Michel said.

"And I yours."

"What is it that I am to do?"

"Just this: dictate to me, in a slow, clear voice, the various quotations from the papers which I am to transfer into the Ledger. Mind what you are about! Speak emphatically, and breathe deeply. There must be no errors—one erasure and I am dismissed."

There were no further preliminaries, and the work began.

Quinsonnas was a young man of thirty who by dint of his serious expression might pass for forty. Yet attentive scrutiny might ultimately discern, beneath that ominous gravity, a good deal of secret joviality and a dash of diabolic wit. Michel, after three days, began to notice something of the kind.

Yet the bookkeeper's reputation for simplicity, not to say stupidity, was celebrated throughout the offices; stories were told about him that would have made the Calinos of the period turn pale! Nonetheless, his splendid calligraphy and his exactitude were indisputable virtues; it was on account of the latter, thanks to his proverbial obtuseness, that he had escaped the two tasks so burdensome for a clerk: jury duty and National Guard service (these two great institutions were still functioning in the year of grace 1960).

Here are the circumstances in which Quinsonnas was removed from the lists of the former and the roll books of the latter. About a year earlier, fate had placed his name in the jury pool; the case was an extremely serious one in the Assize Court and particularly long as well; it had already lasted some eight days, and only now was there some hope of bringing it to an end; the last witnesses were being questioned, but Quinsonnas had not been taken into consideration. In the middle of the session, he stood up and asked the presiding magistrate if the defendant might be asked one question. Permission was granted, the question was asked, and the defendant provided an answer.

"In that case," said Quinsonnas, very loudly, "it is plain that the defendant is not guilty." The effect can be imagined! It is forbidden for any member of the jury to express an opinion during the course of the interrogation, on pain of mistrial! Quinsonnas's blunder thus extended the case to yet another session! And everything had to be started all over again; and since the incorrigible juror, involuntarily or else naively repeated the error, no verdict could be reached!

What could anyone say to the unfortunate Quinsonnas? He was evidently speaking out despite himself, in the heat of the interrogation; his thoughts got the best of him. It was an infirmity, but finally, since Justice had to proceed on its course, he was permanently excused from the jury lists.

The National Guard was another matter. The first time Quinsonnas was assigned to sentry duty at the gates of his municipal district, he took his duties seriously; he stood at attention before his box, his rifle loaded, his finger on the trigger, ready to fire as if the enemy was about to appear around the corner. Naturally some people stared at this zealous sentry—more than a few, in fact; several innocent bystanders smiled. This was not to the fierce National Guardsman's liking. He arrested one, then two, then three of these idlers; at the end of his two hours on duty, he had filled the post. His actions nearly caused a riot.

What could be said? Quinsonnas was quite within his rights; he claimed to have been insulted while under arms! The religion of the flag was on his side, and the incident was inevitably repeated during his next session on duty, and since neither his zeal nor his susceptibility, both quite honorable, after all, could be moderated, he was removed from the military roles.

Quinsonnas may well have passed for an imbecile, yet in this fashion he had managed to avoid both jury duty and National Guard service. Released from these two social burdens, Quinsonnas became a model bookkeeper.

For a month, Michel dictated according to the regulations. His work was easy enough, but it left him not a moment's freedom; Quinsonnas wrote, sometimes shooting a remarkably sharp glance at young Dufrénoy when the latter began declaiming the Ledger's articles in emotional accents.

"What an odd chap," he mused; "yet he seems born for better things! I wonder why he's been put here, being Boutardin's nephew and all? Could it be to take my place? Impossible—he writes like the cook's cat! Maybe he's really just the simpleton he seems. I must get to the bottom of this!"

For his part, Michel indulged in identical reflections: "This Quinsonnas must be playing a double game. Obviously he's born for better things than making those *F*'s or those *M*'s. There are times when I can actually hear him laughing to himself! What's he thinking about?"

Thus these two comrades of the Ledger observed each other; they did so with a clear, frank gaze on either side, thereby generating a communicative spark. Such a situation could not continue without some consequence. Quinsonnas was dying to ask questions, and Michel to answer them, and one fine day, without knowing why, in an expansive mood, Michel was led to tell his life story; he did so excitedly, his words full of feelings that had been repressed too long. Quinsonnas was very likely moved, for he squeezed his young companion's hand. "But your father?" he asked.

"Was a musician."

"A musician—was he that Dufrénoy whose last works are among the finest things in modern music?"

"That was certainly my father."

"A man of genius!" Quinsonnas exclaimed, "a poor man and little known, my dear boy, yet he was my own master!"

"Your master!" Michel gaped.

"Yes, mine!" exclaimed Quinsonnas, brandishing his pen, "to the devil with scruples! *Io son pittore!* I am a musician!"

"You're an artist!"

"Yes, but not so loud! I'll get myself thanked for it," Quinsonnas whispered, quelling the young man's gestures of surprise and delight.

"But . . ."

"Here I'm a bookkeeper; the copyist feeds the musician, until . . ." Here he broke off, staring hard at Michel.

"Until . . ."

"Until the moment I've discovered some practical notion!"

"In industry!" Michel replied, disappointed.

"No, my boy," Quinsonnas replied in a fatherly tone, "in music."

"In music?"

"Silence! Don't question me, it's a secret. I'm going to astound the age. Don't laugh! Laughter is punishable by death these days; our contemporaries are serious to the end of time."

"Astound the age," the young man repeated quite mechanically.

"That's my motto," Quinsonnas answered. "Astound, since I can no longer beguile. Like you, I was born a century too late; and you must do as I do, work! Earn your bread, since all of us must achieve that ignoble thing: digestion! I'll teach you something about life, if you're willing to learn; for fifteen years I've been feeding my poor self quite meagerly, and it's taken strong teeth to chew what fate has put in my mouth! But finally, with a strong pair of jaws, you can get the best of fate! Luckily I fell into a job, of sorts; I have a good hand, as they say. Lord! If I were to lose an arm, what would I do? No piano—no Ledger either! Bah, in time I could learn to play with my feet! I've thought about it. Certainly that's one thing that would astound the age . . ."

Michel couldn't keep from laughing.

"Don't laugh, wretch, it's forbidden chez Casmodage! Look, I have a face that can break stones and an expression that would freeze the Tuileries pond in midsummer. I suppose you've heard how some American philanthropists thought up the idea of throwing their prisoners into round cells so as to deny them even the distraction of corners? Well, my boy, this society of ours is as round as those American jails! A man can gloom away his whole life—"

"But, Monsieur," Michel interrupted, "it seems to me there's something cheerful about you—"

"Not here! Once I'm home, that's different. You come and see me! I'll play you some music—real music! The old kind!"

"Whenever you like," Michel answered, delighted. "But I'd have to get some time off . . ."

"Fine! I'll say you need dictation lessons. But no more of these subversive conversations here! I'm a cog, you're a cog! Let's do our cog work and get back to the litanies of Holy Accountancy!"

"Petty Cash," Michel intoned.

"Petty Cash," Quinsonnas repeated.

And their labor began again. From this day on, young Dufrénoy's existence was noticeably altered; he had a friend; he talked; he could be understood, happy as a mute who has regained the use of his tongue. The

Ledger's summits no longer seemed deserted peaks, and he had no difficulty breathing at such altitudes. Soon the two comrades indulged in the most intimate forms of address.

Quinsonnas shared with Michel all the acquisitions of his experience, and Michel, during his sleepless nights, brooded upon the disappointments of this world; each morning he returned to the offices inflamed by his thoughts of the night before and poured out his thoughts to the musician, who failed to keep him silent. Soon the Ledger was no longer under discussion. "You're going to make us commit some terrible error," Quinsonnas kept saying, "and we'll be thrown out!"

"But I have to talk," Michel answered.

"All right," Quinsonnas said to him one day, "you come and have dinner at my place tonight, with my friend Jacques Aubanet."

"At your place! But we have to get permission . . ."

"I've got it. Where were we?"

"Liquidations," Michel intoned.

"Liquidations," Quinsonnas repeated.

CHAPTER VII

Three Drones

As soon as the bank closed, the two friends headed for Quinsonnas's residence, in the Rue Grange-aux-Belles; they walked arm in arm, Michel exulting in his freedom, his steps those of a conqueror.

It is a good distance from Casmodage and Co. to the Rue Grange-aux-Belles; but lodgings were hard to find in a capital too small for its five million inhabitants; enlarging public squares, opening avenues, and multiplying boulevards threatened to leave little room for private dwellings. Which justified this bromide of the period: in Paris there are no longer houses, only streets!

Some neighborhoods offered no lodging whatever to inhabitants of the capital, specifically the Ile de la Cité, where there was room only for the Bureau of Commerce, the Palace of Justice, the Prefecture of Police, the cathedral, the morgue—in other words, the means of being declared bankrupt, guilty, jailed, buried, and even rescued. Public buildings had driven out houses.

That accounted for the high cost of present-day lodgings; the Imperial Real Estate Corporation was gradually seizing all of Paris, in collusion with the government-controlled Building Company, and yielded magnificent dividends. This corporation, founded by two skillful financiers of the nineteenth century, the brothers Péreire, now also owned many of the chief cities of France, Lyons, Marseilles, Bordeaux, Nantes, Strasbourg, Lille, which it had gradually rebuilt. Its shares, which had split five times, were still quoted on the Bourse at 4,450 francs.

Poorer people reluctant to live far from the center of town therefore had to live high up; what they gained in proximity they lost in elevation—a matter of fatigue, henceforth, and not of time.

Quinsonnas lived in a twelfth-floor walk-up, an old apartment house which would have been greatly improved by elevator service. But once he was at home, the musician found himself no worse for wear.

When they reached the Rue Grange-aux-Belles, he dashed up the huge spiral staircase. "Don't think about it—just keep climbing," he panted to Michel, who was following just behind him. "We'll get there eventually—nothing is eternal in this world, not even stairs. There!" he gasped, flinging open his door after a breathtaking ascent.

He pushed the young man into his "apartments," a single room some fourteen meters square. "No vestibule!" he observed. "That's for people who want to keep other people waiting, and since most visitors and salespeople seem a good deal less eager to climb twelve flights than to walk down them, I do without; I've also done without a living room, which would have made the lack of a dining room too obvious."

"It looks fine to me," said Michel, once he had caught his breath.

"At least the air is as fresh as the ammonia of Paris mud permits."

"It only seems small at first glance," said Michel.

"And at second, but it'll do."

"Besides, it's so well arranged," Michel continued, laughing.

"Well now, you old darling," Quinsonnas remarked to an elderly woman who came in just then, "is dinner on the way? We'll be three starving guests tonight."

"On its way, Monsieur Quinsonnas," replied the crone, "but you know I couldn't set the table—there is no table!"

"We'll do without," Michel exclaimed, rather enjoying the prospect of dining on his lap.

"What do you mean, we'll do without!" interjected Quinsonnas. "Can you suppose I'd invite friends to dinner without having a table to serve it on?"

"I don't see . . . ," began Michel, glancing dubiously around the room, which indeed contained neither table, nor bed, nor armoire, nor commode, nor chair. Not one piece of furniture, except for a good-sized piano.

"You don't see . . . ," repeated Quinsonnas. "Well now! What about industry, that kind mother, and mechanics, that fine young lady, are you forgetting them? Here is the table as requested." With these words he went over to the piano, pressed a button, and there sprang forth—no other words were adequate to the occasion—a table fitted with benches at which three guests could sit with plenty of room.

"Very ingenious," Michel observed.

"Necessity is our mother," the pianist replied, "since the exiguity of the apartments no longer permitted furniture! Have a look at this complex instrument, an amalgamation of Érard and Jeanselme! It fills every need, takes up no room at all, and I can assure you that the piano itself is none the worse for it."

At this moment the doorbell rang. Quinsonnas opened the door and announced his friend Jacques

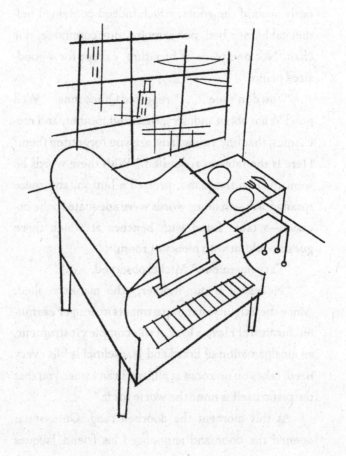

Aubanet, an employee of the General Corporation of Maritime Mines. Michel and Jacques were introduced to each other in the simplest manner possible.

Jacques Aubanet, a handsome young man of twenty-five, was a close friend of Quinsonnas, and like him reduced in circumstances. Michel had no idea what kind of work the employees of the Corporation of Maritime Mines might do; certainly Jacques brought with him a remarkable appetite.

Fortunately dinner was ready; the three young men *devoured*: after the initial moments of this struggle with comestibles, a few words managed to make their way through the less expeditive mouthfuls. "My dear Jacques," Quinsonnas observed, "by introducing you to Michel Dufrénoy I allowed you to make the acquaintance of a young friend who is one of us— one of those poor devils Society refuses to employ according to their talents, one of those drones whose useless mouths Society padlocks in order not to have to feed!"

"Ah! Monsieur Dufrénoy is a dreamer," Jacques replied.

"A poet, my friend! and I wonder what in the world he can be doing here in Paris, where a man's first duty is to make money!"

"Obviously enough," Jacques replied, "he's landed on the wrong planet."

"My friends," said Michel, "you're anything but encouraging, but I shall take your exaggerations into account."

"This dear child," Quinsonnas replied, "he hopes, he works, he loves good books, and when Hugo, Musset, and Lamartine are no longer read, he hopes someone will still read *him*! But what have you done, wretch that you are—have you invented a utilitarian poetry, a literature to replace compressed air or power brakes? No? Well then! Gnaw your own vitals, my son! If you don't have something sensational to tell, who will listen to you? Art is no longer possible unless it produces a tour de force! These days, Hugo would have to recite his *Orientales* straddling two circus horses, and Lamartine would perform his *Harmonies* upside down from a trapeze!"

"Nonsense," exclaimed Michel, leaping up in indignation.

"Calm down, child," the pianist replied. "Just ask Jacques whether I'm right or not."

"A hundred times over," Jacques opined. "This world is nothing more than a market, an immense fairground, and you must entertain your clients with the talents of a mountebank."

"Poor Michel," Quinsonnas continued with a sigh, "his Latin verse prize will turn his head!"

"What will you prove by that?" demanded the young man.

"Nothing, my son! After all, you're following your destiny. You're a great poet! I've seen some of your works; only you'll allow me to remark that they're hardly suited to the taste of the age."

"Which means?"

"Which means that you deal with poetical subjects, and nowadays that's a poetical fault! You sing of mountains and valleys, fields and clouds, love and the stars—all those worn-out things no one wants anymore!"

"Then what should I sing?"

"Your verses must celebrate the wonders of industry!"

"Never!" Michel exclaimed.

"Well put," Jacques observed.

"For instance," Quinsonnas continued, "have you heard the ode that was given first prize by the forty de Broglies cluttering up the Académie-Française?"

"No!"

"Well then, listen and learn. Here are the two last stanzas:

And coal was shoveled into blazing fires:
Through glowing tubes the pressure it requires
Is driven to the monster's heart; it pumps
In pulsing fury and in frenzy thumps
Till, bellowing, it emulates the forces
                              of eighty horses!

Now with his heavy bars, the engineer
Opens the valves! Within the cylinder
The double piston runs! The wheel has slipped
Its cog! The roaring engine's speed is up!
The whistle blows! . . . Hail to the Crampton System:
                              the locomotive runs!

"Dreadful!" Michel exclaimed.

"Some nice rhymes," Jacques observed.

"There you are, my boy," continued the pitiless Quinsonnas. "May heaven keep you from being forced to live by your talent! Better follow the example of those of us who recognize the present state of affairs for what it is, at least until better days."

"Is Monsieur Jacques," inquired Michel, "similarly obliged to ply some rebarbative trade?"

"Jacques is a shipping clerk in an industrial company," Quinsonnas explained, "which does not mean, to his great regret, that he has ever seen the inside of a ship."

"What does it mean?" asked Michel.

"It means," Jacques replied, "that I'd have liked to be a soldier."

"A soldier!" Michel betrayed his astonishment.

"Yes, a soldier. A noble profession in which, barely fifty years ago, you could earn an honest living!"

"Unless you lost it even more honestly," Quinsonnas added. "Well, it's over and done with as a career, since there's no more army—unless you become a policeman. In other times, Jacques would have entered some military academy, or joined up, and there, after a life of battle, he would have become a general like a Turenne, or an emperor like a Bonaparte! But nowadays, my handsome officer, you'll have to give that all up."

"Oh, you never know!" said Jacques. "It's true that France, England, Russia, and Italy have dismissed their soldiers; during the last century the engines of warfare were perfected to such a degree that the whole thing had become ridiculous—France couldn't help laughing—"

"And having laughed," Quinsonnas put in, "she disarmed."

"Yes, you joker! I grant you that with the exception of old Austria, the European peoples have done away with the military state. But for all that, have they done away with the spirit of battle natural to human beings, and the spirit of conquest natural to governments?"

"Probably," remarked the musician.

"And why?"

"Because the best reason those instincts had for existing was the possibility of satisfying them! Because nothing suggests battle so much as an armed peace, according to the old expression! Because if you do away with painters there's no more painting, sculptors, no more sculpture, musicians, no more music, and if you do away with warriors—no more wars! Soldiers are artists."

"Yes, of course!" Michel exclaimed, "and rather than do the awful work I do, I ought to join up."

"Ah, you fell for it, baby!" Quinsonnas crowed. "Is there any possibility that you'd like to fight?"

"Fighting ennobles the soul," Michel replied, "at least according to Stendhal, one of the great thinkers of the last century."

"Yes, it does," the pianist agreed, but added, "How much brains does it take to give a good thrust with a saber?"

"A lot, if you're going to do it right," Jacques answered.

"And even more, if you're going to receive the thrust," Quinsonnas retorted. "My word, my friends, it's likely you're right, from a certain point of view. Perhaps I'd be inclined to make you a soldier, if there was still an army; with a little philosophy, it's a fine career. But nowadays, since the Champs-de-Mars has been turned into a school, we must give up fighting."

"We'll go back to it," said Jacques; "one fine day, some unexpected complication will arise . . ."

"I don't think so, my brave friend, for our bellicose notions are fading away, and with them our honorable ideas. . . . In France in the old days, men were afraid of ridicule, but do you think such a thing as a point of honor still exists? There are no duels fought nowadays; the fashion is past; we either compromise or we sue; now, if we no longer fight for honor's sake, why should we do it for politics? If individuals no longer take sword in hand, why should governments pull them from the scabbards? Battles were never more numerous than in the days of duels, and if there are no more duelists, then there are no more soldiers."

"Oh, new ones will be born," Jacques declared.

"I doubt it, since the links of commerce are drawing nations ever closer together! The British, the Russians, the Americans all have their banknotes, their rubles, their dollars invested in our commercial enterprises. Isn't money the enemy of the bullet? Hasn't the cotton bale replaced the cannonball? Just think, Jacques! Aren't the British enjoying a privilege they deny us, and gradually becoming the great landowners of France? They possess enormous territories, almost *départements* now, not conquered but bought, which is a lot more permanent! No one realized what was happening, we just let it happen, and soon these foreigners will own our entire country, and that's when they'll take their revenge on William the Conqueror!"

"My dear fellow," Jacques replied, "remember this, and you too, young man, listen to what I say, for it's the century's profession of faith: With Montaigne and maybe Rabelais it was What Do I Know? In the nineteenth century it was What Does It Matter to Me? And nowadays we say: How Much Does It Earn? Well, the day a war earns as much as an industrial investment, then there'll be wars."

"Good! War has never earned anything, especially for France."

"Because we fought for honor and not for money," Jacques replied.

"So you believe in an army of intrepid businessmen?"

"Of course. Look at the Americans in their dreadful War of Secession."

"Well, my friend, an army that fights for a financial motive will no longer be composed of soldiers, but of looters and thieves!"

"All the same, such an army will accomplish wonders."

"Thieving wonders," Quinsonnas put in. And the three young men burst out laughing. "To conclude," resumed the pianist, "here we have Michel, a poet, and Jacques, a soldier, and Quinsonnas, a musician, and this at a moment when our country no longer has music, or poetry, or an army! We are, quite obviously, stupid, all three of us. But at least the meal is over—it was quite substantial, at least in conversation. Let's proceed with other exercises." The table, once cleared, returned to its slots and grooves, and the piano resumed the place of honor.

CHAPTER VIII

Which Concerns Music, Ancient and Modern, and the Practical Utilization of Certain Instruments

"So at last," Michel exclaimed, "we're going to have a little music."

"But not modern music," said Jacques. "It's too hard."

"To understand, yes," Quinsonnas replied, "but not to make."

"How's that?" asked Michel.

"I'll explain," said Quinsonnas, "and I'm going to support what I say with a striking example. Michel, be so good as to open the piano." The young man obliged. "Good. Now, sit down on the keyboard."

"What? You want me . . ."

"Sit down, I said." Michel lowered himself onto the keys of the instrument and produced a jangling clash of sounds. "Do you know what you've just done?" asked the pianist.

"I haven't a clue!"

"Innocent! You've just created modern harmony."

"Right," said Jacques.

"Really, that's a perfect chord for our times, and the awful thing about it is that today's scholars take it upon themselves to explain it scientifically! In the past, only certain notes could be sounded together; but they've been reconciled since then, and now they no longer quarrel among themselves—they're too well brought up for such a thing!"

"But the effect is still just as unpleasant," Jacques put in.

"Well, my friend, we've reached this point by the force of events; in the last century, a certain Richard Wagner, a sort of messiah who has been insufficiently crucified, invented the Music of the Future, and we're still enduring it; in his day, melody was already being suppressed, and he decided it was appropriate to get rid of harmony as well—and the house has remained empty ever since."

"But," Michel reflected, "it's as if you were making a painting without drawing or color!"

"Precisely," replied Quinsonnas. "And now that you've mentioned painting—painting isn't really a French art, it comes to us from Italy and from Germany, and I would suffer less seeing it profaned. But music is the very daughter of our heart . . ."

"I thought," said Jacques, "that music started in Italy!"

"A mistake, my son; until the middle of the sixteenth century, French music dominated Europe; the Huguenot Goudimel was Palestrina's teacher, and the oldest as well as the most naive melodies are Gallic."

"And now we've reached this point," said Michel.

"Yes, my son; on the pretext that we are following new formulas, a score now consists of only a single phrase—long, loopy, endless. At the Opéra, it begins at eight o'clock and ends just before midnight; if it should extend five minutes more, it costs the management a fine and overtime for the house workers."

"And this happens without protest?"

"My son, music is no longer tasted, it is swallowed! A few artists put up a struggle, among them your father; but since his death, not a single note has been written worthy of that name! Either we endure the nauseating *melody of the virgin forest,* insipid, confused, indeterminate, or else various harmony rackets are produced, of which you have given us such a touching example by sitting on the piano."

"Pathetic!" said Michel.

"Horrible!" replied Jacques.

"Also, my friends," Quinsonnas resumed, "you must have observed what big ears we have!"

"No," replied Jacques.

"Well then, just compare our ears with those of the ancients and with the ears of the Middle Ages—examine the paintings and statues, measure the results, and you will be astonished! Ears grow in proportion as the human body shrinks: someday the final result will be something to see! Well, my friends, physiologists have been diligent in searching out the cause of this decadence, and it seems that it is music we have to thank for such appendages; we are living in an age of wizened tympanums and distorted hearing. You realize that no one keeps a century of Verdi or Wagner in his ears without that organ's having to pay for it."

"That Quinsonnas is a terrifying devil," said Jacques.

"Nonetheless," Michel replied, "the old masterpieces are still performed at the Opéra."

"I know," Quinsonnas answered; "there's even some talk of reviving Offenbach's *Orpheus in the Underworld* with the recitatives Gounod added to that masterpiece, and it's quite possible that the production will even make a little money, on account of the ballet! What our enlightened public requires, my friends, is some dancing! When you think that a monument costing twenty million francs has been erected chiefly to allow some jumping jacks to be maneuvered around the stage. . . . They've cut *Les Huguenots* to a single act,

and this little curtain-raiser accompanies the fashion-
able ballets; the dancers' costumes have been made
transparent enough to deceive nature herself, and this
enlivens our financiers; the Opéra, moreover, has become a branch of the Bourse—quite as much screaming
goes on there; business is conducted in full voice, and
no one bothers much about the music! Between us,
I must admit, the execution leaves something to be
desired."

"A great deal to be desired," Jacques replied. "The
singers whinny, cackle, shriek, and bray—anything and
everything but sing. A menagerie!"

"As for the orchestra," Quinsonnas continued, "it
has fallen very low since his instrument no longer suf-
fices to feed the instrumentalist! Talk about a trade
that's not practical! Ah, if we could use the power
wasted on the pedals of a piano for pumping water out
of coal mines! If the air escaping from ophicleides
could also be used to turn the Catacomb Company's
windmills! If the trombone's alternating action could
be applied to a mechanical sawmill—oh, then the exe-
cutants would be rich and many!"

"You're joking," exclaimed Michel.

"God help me," replied Quinsonnas quite seriously, "I shouldn't be surprised if some ingenious in-

ventor managed such things one day! The spirit of invention is what is highly developed in France nowadays! It's really the only spirit we have left! And I can tell you it doesn't make conversations very lively! But who dreams of being entertained? Let's bore one another to death! That's our ruling principle today!"

"And you can't see any remedy for it?" Michel asked.

"None, so long as finance and machinery prevail! And it's really machinery that's doing the mischief."

"Why is that?"

"Because there's this one good thing about finance: at least it can pay for masterpieces, and a man must eat, even if he has genius! The Genoese, the Venetians, the Florentines under Lorenzo the Magnificent, bankers and businessmen as they were, all encouraged the arts! But mechanics, engineers, technicians—devil take me if Raphael, Titian, Veronese, and Leonardo could ever have come into being! They'd have had to compete with mechanical procedures, and they'd have starved to death! Ah, machinery! It's enough to make you loathe inventors and inventions alike!"

"But after all," said Michel, "you're a musician, Quinsonnas, you work! You spend your nights at your piano—do you refuse to play modern music?"

"Oh, me! I play as much of it as anyone else—here's a piece I've just written that will appeal to today's taste; it may even have some success, if it finds a publisher."

"What are you calling it?"

"After Thilorier—a Grand Fantasy on the Liquefaction of Carbonic Acid."

"You can't be serious!" Michel exclaimed.

"Listen and judge for yourselves," Quinsonnas replied. He sat down at the piano, or rather he flung himself at it. Under his fingers, under his hands, under his elbows, the wretched instrument produced impossible sounds; notes collided and crackled like hailstones. No melody, no rhythm! The artist had undertaken to portray the final experiment which had cost Thilorier his life.

"There!" he exclaimed. "Did you hear that? Now do you understand? Are you aware of the great chemist's experiment? Have you been taken into his laboratory? Do you feel how the carbonic acid is separated out? Here we have a pressure of four hundred ninety-five atmospheres! The cylinder is turning—watch out! watch out! The machine is going to explode! Take cover!" And with a blow of his fist capable of splintering the ivory keys, Quinsonnas reproduced the explosion. "Whew!" he said, "isn't that imitative enough—isn't that beautiful?"

Michel remained stupefied. Jacques couldn't help laughing.

"And you expect a lot from a piece like that," he said.

"Expect a lot!" Quinsonnas replied. "It's of my time—everyone's a chemist nowadays. I'll be understood. Only it isn't enough to have ideas, there must be proper execution."

"What do you mean?" asked Jacques.

"Just what I said. It's by execution that I plan to astound the age."

"But it sounds to me," Michel argued, "as if you played that piece wonderfully."

"Don't be ridiculous," said the artist with a shrug of his shoulders. "I haven't mastered the first note, though I've been studying the cursed thing for three years!"

"What more do you want to do with it?"

"That's my secret, my children; don't ask me to share it with you, you'd only think I was mad, and that would discourage me. But I can assure you that one day the talents of Liszt and Thalberg, of Prudent and of Schulhoff, will be exposed for what they are."

"You mean you want to play three more notes per second than they do?" asked Jacques.

"No, but I'll be playing the piano in a new way, a way that will amaze the public! How? I can't tell you.

One allusion, one indiscretion, and someone will steal my idea from me. The vile pack of imitators will be on my heels, and I want to be unique. But that requires superhuman labor! When I'm sure of myself my fortune will be made, and I'll say farewell to Bookkeeping forever!"

"I really think you must be mad," said Jacques.

"No, not mad, merely maniacal, which is what you must be in order to succeed! But let's get back to some gentler feelings and try to revive a little of that charming past for which we were born too late. Here, my friends, is truth in music!"

Quinsonnas was a great artist; he played with profound feeling, and he knew everything the preceding centuries had bequeathed to his own, which refused the legacy! He took the art at its birth, passing rapidly from master to master, and by his rather rough but sympathetic voice completed what his fingers' execution lacked. He passed in review before his delighted friends the whole history of music, from Rameau and Lully to Mozart and on to Beethoven and Weber, illustrating all the founders of the art, weeping with the gentle inspirations of Grétry, and triumphing in the splendid pages of Rossini and Meyerbeer. "Listen!" he said, "here are the forgotten songs of *Guillaume Tell,* of *Robert le Diable,* of *Les Huguenots;* here is the charming period of Hérold and Auber, two learned men who did themselves honor by knowing nothing! Ah, what has knowledge to do with music? Has it any access to painting? No, and painting and music are all one! That is how people understood this great art during the first half of the nineteenth century! They didn't search out new formulas—there's nothing new to find in music, any more than in love. It remains the charming prerogative of the sensuous arts to be eternally young!"

"Bravo!" cried Jacques.

"But then," the pianist continued, "certain ambitious natures felt the need to follow new and unknown paths, and they have dragged music after them . . . into the abyss!"

"Are you saying," Michel asked, "that you no longer count a single composer after Meyerbeer and Rossini as a true musician?"

"Not at all!" answered Quinsonnas, boldly modulating from D natural to E flat; "I'm not talking about Berlioz, leader of that impotent troupe whose musical ideas were packaged in envious feuilletons; but here are some of the heirs of the great masters: listen to Félicien David, a specialist whom our contemporary experts take for King David, first harpist of the Hebrews! Savor those true and simple inspirations of Massé, the last musician of heart and feeling, who in his *Indienne* has given us the masterpiece of his period! Then there's Gounod, the splendid composer of *Faust* who died soon after having taken orders in the Wagnerian church. And then Verdi, the man of harmonic noise, the hero of musical racket, who made wholesale melody the way certain writers of the period made wholesale literature—Verdi, creator of the inexhaustible *Trovatore*, who played his singular part in distorting the century's taste . . .

Enfin Wagnerbe vint . . ."

At this moment, Quinsonnas let his fingers, no longer constrained by any recognizable rhythm, wander into the incomprehensible reveries of Contemplative Music, proceeding by abrupt intervals and disappearing into the midst of an endless phrase.

With incomparable talent the artist had evidenced the successive gradations of his art; two hundred years of music had just passed beneath his fingers, and his friends listened to him, mute and marveling. Suddenly, in the midst of a powerful elucubration on the Wagnerian school, at the moment when thought was vanishing, dismayed, with no hope of returning to its true path, when sounds gradually gave way to noises whose musical value was no longer appreciable—suddenly a

simple, melodic piece, of gentle character and perfectly apt feeling, began to sing beneath the pianist's
fingers. This was the calm after the storm, the heart's
true note after so much wailing and roaring.

"Ah!" Jacques smiled.

"My friends," Quinsonnas resumed, "there is still
one great unknown artist who alone epitomized the
genius of all music. This piece dates from 1947, and it is
the last sigh of expiring art."

"And it's by . . . ?" Michel asked.

"It's by your father, who was my beloved master."

"My father!" the young man exclaimed, nearly in
tears.

"Yes. Listen." And Quinsonnas, reproducing
melodies which Beethoven or Weber would have been
proud to sign, rose to the sublime heights of interpre-
tation.

"My father!" Michel repeated.

"Yes!" Quinsonnas replied, closing his piano with
contained fury. "After him, nothing! Who would understand his music now? Enough, my sons—enough of
this return to the past! Let us remember the present,
our present, when industrialism has come into its own,
its empire, its triumph!" And with these words he
touched the instrument, whereupon the keyboard
folded up and in its place revealed a bed entirely made

up, with a well-stocked night table attached to one side. "Now this," he said, "is what our epoch was worthy of inventing! A piano-bed-dresser-commode!"

"And night table as well," Jacques added.

"Just as you say, my dear fellow. That puts the lid on it!"

CHAPTER IX

A Visit to Uncle Huguenin

Since that memorable evening, the three young men had become close friends; they constituted a little world of their own in the vast capital of France.

Michel spent his days on the Ledger, apparently resigned to his work, though his happiness was spoiled by not having time to visit Uncle Huguenin, with whom he would have felt in the bosom of a veritable family, having his uncle for father and his two friends for elder brothers. He wrote frequently to the old librarian, who replied almost as often.

Four months passed in this fashion; Michel evidently gave satisfaction in the offices; his cousin treated him a little less scornfully; Quinsonnas praised him to the skies. The young man had apparently found his way—he was born to dictate.

Winter passed, stoves and gas heaters mustered to combat it with success. And spring arrived. Michel obtained a whole day's freedom, a Sunday, and resolved to spend it with Uncle Huguenin. At eight in the morning he gaily left the bank building, delighted to breathe more oxygen away from the central business district. The weather was splendid. April was awakening and preparing its new flowers, with which the florists waged advantageous combat; Michel felt very much alive.

His uncle lived far away, having had to transport his Penates where it did not cost too much to shelter them. Young Dufrénoy proceeded to the Madeleine station, took his ticket, and hoisted himself onto an upper-level seat; the signal for departure sounded, and the train moved up the Boulevard Malesherbes, soon leaving on its right the heavily ornamented church of Saint-Augustin and on its left the Parc Monceau, surrounded by splendid edifices; it crossed the two Metropolitan rings and stopped at the Porte d'Asnières station, near the old fortifications. The first part of the journey was over: Michel leaped down and followed the Rue d'Asnières as far as the Rue de la Révolte, turned left, passing under the Versailles Railway, and finally reached the corner of the Rue du Caillou. Here stood an apartment house of modest appearance, high and densely inhabited; he asked the concierge for Monsieur Huguenin.

"Ninth floor, first door to your right," responded this important personage, a government employee directly appointed to this confidential position. Michel thanked him, took his place in the elevator, and in a few seconds was standing on the ninth-floor landing. He rang. Monsieur Huguenin himself came to the door.

"Uncle!" exclaimed Michel.

"My dear boy!" the old man replied, throwing wide his arms. "Here you are at last."

"Yes, Uncle, and my first free day is for you!"

"Thank you, my boy," replied Monsieur Huguenin, leading the young man into his apartment. "What a pleasure to see you! But sit down, let me have your hat, make yourself comfortable—you'll stay awhile, won't you?"

"All day, Uncle, if it's no trouble for you."

"Trouble! My dear boy, I've been waiting for you all this time!"

"Waiting! But I really haven't had time to let you know in advance—I'd have got here before my letter."

"I expected you each Sunday, Michel, and your place has always been set at the table, as it is now."

"Can this be possible?"

"I knew perfectly well you'd be coming to see your uncle one day or another. Till now, it's always been another."

"I wasn't free, Uncle."

"I know you weren't, my boy, and I'm not in the least put out about that; far from it."

"How happy you must be, living here," said Michel, glancing enviously around him.

"You're looking at these old friends of mine, my books! All in good time, but let's begin with some lunch; we'll talk about all this later, though I promised myself I wouldn't discuss literature with you."

"Oh, Uncle, please!" Michel pleaded.

"We'll see! There are other things to discuss! Tell me what you're doing, how you're getting on in that bank! Are your ideas . . . ?"

"Still the same, Uncle."

"The devil you say! Let's sit down, then! But it seems to me you haven't yet given me a hug."

"Not yet, Uncle, not yet!"

"Now let's begin all over again, Nephew! It can't do me any harm, I haven't eaten yet; in fact, it will give me an appetite."

Michel embraced his uncle with all his heart, and the two took their places at the table. Yet the young man kept staring around him, for there was every reason to appeal to his poet's curiosity. The little salon which, along with a bedroom, formed the whole apartment was lined with books; the walls were quite invisible behind the shelves; old bindings attracted Michel's gaze, their warm colors embrowned by time. And books had even invaded the next room, ranked over doors and inside the window bays; there were books on all the furniture, around the fireplace, even on the floors of the gaping cupboards; these precious volumes bore little resemblance to the opulent but useless libraries of the rich; they seemed instead to be at home, masters of the place, and quite at ease, though often in towering piles; moreover, there was not a speck of dust anywhere, not a corner of a page was turned down, no stain marred the fine covers; it was apparent that a friendly hand had prepared their ablutions each morning.

Two old armchairs and a table dating back to the days of the Empire with gilded sphinxes and Roman fasces constituted the salon's furnishings.

Though the room enjoyed a southern exposure, a courtyard's high walls kept the sun from penetrating very far—only once a year, at the summer solstice on June 21, if the weather was fine, the highest sunbeam brushed the neighboring roof and slid through the window, coming to rest like a bird on the corner of a shelf or the back of a book, shimmered there a moment, its luminous projection tingeing the tiny atoms of dust; then, after a moment, it resumed its flight and vanished until the following year.

Uncle Huguenin knew this shelf, always the same one, quite well; he watched it, heart pounding, with an astronomer's attention; he bathed in its beneficent light, set his old clock according to its passage, and thanked the sun for not having forgotten him. This was his own version of the Palais-Royal cannon, except that it went off only once a year, and not always then! Uncle Huguenin did not forget to invite Michel to make a solemn visit on June 21, and Michel promised to be there for the celebration.

Lunch was on the table, modest but enthusiastically served. "This is my gala day," the uncle remarked, "today is my treat. By the way, do you know with whom you're dining this evening?"

"No, Uncle."

"With your old Professor Richelot and his granddaughter, Mademoiselle Lucy."

"My word, Uncle! What a pleasure it will be for me to see that good man."

"And Mademoiselle Lucy?"

"I don't know her."

"Well, Nephew, you'll make her acquaintance, and I can tell you she's a charming creature, and no mistake! So there's no need to tell her as much," Uncle Huguenin added with a laugh.

"I'll be careful not to."

"After dinner, if you like, the four of us can go for a stroll."

"Just what I'd like, Uncle! That way, our day will be complete!"

"You're not eating any more, Michel. Won't you have something more to drink?"

"Certainly, Uncle," replied Michel, who was feeling full. "To your health."

"And to your next visit, my boy; for when you leave here, it still seems like a long journey to me! Now tell me something about yourself—how is life treating you these days? You see, this is the moment for confidences."

"I'm glad it is, Uncle."

Michel described at some length all the details of his existence, his problems, his poor performance with regard to the calculating machine, without omitting the episode of the self-defending safe, and finally the better days spent on the heights of the Ledger. "It was up there that I met my first friend."

"Ah, you have friends," Uncle Huguenin remarked with a frown.

"I have two."

"That's a good many, if they deceive you," the old fellow remarked sententiously, "and enough, if they love you."

"Oh, Uncle," Michel exclaimed with animation. "They're artists!"

"Yes," Uncle Huguenin replied, tossing his head, "that's a guarantee of a sort: the statistics of prisons and reformatories include priests, lawyers, brokers, and bankers, and not a single artist! But—"

"You'll meet them, Uncle, and you'll see what splendid fellows they are!"

"I look forward to it," Uncle Huguenin answered. "I love youth, provided it's young! These premature old men of ours have always struck me as hypocrites."

"Oh, I can answer for these two."

"Then judging from your associations, Michel, I should guess your ideas haven't changed?"

"Quite the contrary, Uncle."

"You've become a hardened sinner!"

"Yes, Uncle, I have."

"All right then, wretch, confess your latest trespasses."

"Gladly, Uncle!" And in an enthusiastic tone the young man recited some fine verses of his own composition, carefully thought out, nicely spoken, and filled with a true spirit of poetry.

"Bravo!" exclaimed Uncle Huguenin, transported. "Bravo, my boy! So such things are still being written. You speak the language of the good old days! O my boy, how much pleasure you give me, along with how much pain!" The old man and the young one remained silent for a few moments. "Enough of that!" said Uncle Huguenin. "Let's clear this table, which is getting in our way!" Michel helped the old man, and the dining room swiftly became a library once more.

"Now, Uncle?" inquired Michel.

CHAPTER X

Grand Review of French Authors Conducted by Uncle Huguenin, Sunday, April 15, 1961

"This will be our dessert," said Uncle Huguenin, gesturing toward the crowded shelves.

"It gives me an appetite all over again," Michel replied. "Let's dig in."

Uncle and nephew, each as young as the other, began rummaging among the shelves, in twenty places at once, though Monsieur Huguenin lost no time in restoring some order to this pillage.

"Come over here," he said to Michel, "and let's begin at the beginning; we're not going to read today, we'll just look and talk. This is a review, rather than a battle. Think of yourself as Napoleon in the Tuileries courtyard, and not on the field of Austerlitz. Put your hands behind your back. We're going to pass through the ranks."

"I'm following you, Uncle."

"My boy, remember that the finest army in the world is about to parade before your eyes; there is no other nation which can offer such a sight, and which has won such brilliant victories over barbarism."

"The Grand Army of Letters."

"There on that first shelf, uniformed in their fine morocco bindings, stand our old sixteenth-century veterans, Amyot, Ronsard, Rabelais, Montaigne, Mathurin Régnier; they're staunch at their positions, and you can still detect their original influence in the fine French language they established. But it must be admitted that they fought harder for ideas than for form. Here's a general close by who fought with great valor, though he mainly perfected the weapons of his day."

"Malherbe!"

"Himself. As he says somewhere, the picklocks of Port-au-Foin were his masters; he gleaned their metaphors, their eminently Gallic expressions, he cleaned them, polished them, and out of them made that splendid language spoken so handsomely in the seventeenth, eighteenth, and nineteenth centuries."

"Ah!" said Michel, pointing to a single volume proudly and simply bound, "now there's a great captain."

"Yes, my boy, like Alexander, Caesar, or Napoleon: indeed Bonaparte would have made Corneille a prince!

The old warrior has astonishingly multiplied, for his classical editions are countless; this is the fifty-first and last of his complete works, dating from 1873; since then, Corneille has never been reprinted."

"You must have gone to a great deal of trouble, Uncle, to have obtained all these works!"

"On the contrary—everyone was getting rid of them! Look, here's the forty-ninth edition of the complete works of Racine, the hundred fiftieth of Molière, the fortieth of Pascal, the two hundred third of La Fontaine, the last actually, and they date from over a hundred years ago and already constitute the delight of bibliophiles! These geniuses have served their time, and now they're relegated to the rank of archaeological specimens."

"And in fact," replied the young man, "they speak a language no longer understood in this day and age."

"That's quite true, my boy! The fine French tongue has been lost; the language illustrious foreigners like Leibniz, Frederick the Great, Ancillon, Humboldt, and Heine chose as the interpreter of their ideas—that wonderful language Goethe regretted never having written, that elegant idiom which nearly became Greek or Latin in the fifteenth century, Italian with Catherine de Médicis, and Gascon under Henri IV—is now a horrible argot. Each specialist, forgetting that a language is finer in its action than in its accumulation, has created his own word to name his own thing. Botanists, natural historians, physicists, chemists, mathematicians have coined dreadful hybrids, inventors have ransacked the English vocabulary for their most disagreeable appellations; horse traders for their horses, jockeys for their races, carriage dealers for their vehicles, philosophers for their philosophy—all of them have found the French language too poor and have resorted to foreigners! Well, let them! Let them forget all about it! French is even lovelier in its poverty and hasn't tried to grow rich by prostituting herself! Our own language, my boy, the language of Malherbe, and Molière, of Bossuet and Voltaire, of Nodier and Victor Hugo, is a well-brought-up young lady, and you need have no fear when you fall in love with her, for the barbarians of the twentieth century have failed to turn her into a courtesan!"

"How eloquent you are, Uncle—now I understand the delightful mania of old Professor Richelot, whose scorn for modern slang made him speak nothing but a sort of Frenchified Latin! People make fun of him, but he's quite right. . . . All the same, Uncle, hasn't French become the language of diplomacy?"

"Yes! as a punishment! At the Congress of Nijmegen in 1678! Its virtues of directness and clarity caused it to be chosen by diplomacy, which is the science of duplicity, of equivocation and of mendacity, so that our honest language has gradually been diluted and lost! You'll see—people will have to change it someday."

"Poor French!" Michel sighed. "I see Bossuet over there, and Fénelon, and Saint-Simon, who wouldn't recognize it now!"

"Yes, their child has turned out poorly! That's what comes of frequenting scientists, industrialists, diplomats, and other bad company. Dissipation! Debauchery! A 1960 dictionary that wants to include all terms in use is twice the size of an 1800 dictionary! As for what is to be found there, I leave that to your imagination. But let's return to our review—soldiers shouldn't be kept under arms too long."

"I see a long row of fine volumes over there."

"Fine and sometimes good," Uncle Huguenin answered. "That's the four hundred twenty-eighth edition of the individual works of Voltaire: a universal mind, second in every genre, according to Monsieur Joseph Prudhomme. In 1978, according to Stendhal, Voltaire will be Voiture, and the dimwits will be making him their god. Fortunately Stendhal put too much faith in the future. Dimwits? There are no wits at all nowadays, and Voltaire is worshiped no more than any other . . . god. To continue our metaphor, Voltaire, as

I see him, was only an armchair general! He gave battle orders in his study, and didn't really see how the land lay. His wit, actually not so dangerous a weapon, occasionally misfired, and the people he killed often outlived him."

"But, Uncle, wasn't he a great writer?"

"Certainly, Nephew—he was the French language incarnate, and wielded it with elegance and spirit—the way those regimental instructors used to aim at the wall during fencing instruction: when it came to actual duels, the first clumsy conscript who lunged past his guard managed to kill the fencing master. In short—and this is really surprising for a man who wrote French so well—Voltaire was not really a brave man."

"I guess not," said Michel.

"Let's move on to others," said Uncle Huguenin, heading for a dark and severe line of soldiers.

"There are your authors of the late eighteenth century," the young man observed.

"Yes, Rousseau, who said the finest things about the Gospels, just as Robespierre wrote the most remarkable things about the immortality of the soul! A veritable General of the Republic, Jean-Jacques, in sabots, without epaulets or gold-embroidered uniforms! Which didn't keep him from winning some proud victories! Look, there's Beaumarchais next to him, an avant-garde sniper judiciously engaged in that great battle of '89, which civilization won over barbarism! Unfortunately, that victory has been somewhat abused subsequently, and the devil of Progress has brought us where we are today."

"Perhaps a revolution will be made against Progress . . ."

"Possible, possible, and that would have its amusing aspects. But let's not lose ourselves in such philosophical divagations, Nephew—let's keep on our way through the ranks. Here's a sumptuous commander who spent forty years of his life talking about his modesty: Chateaubriand, and even his *Mémoires d'Outre-Tombe* haven't been able to save him from oblivion."

"Isn't that Bernardin de Saint-Pierre beside him? I suspect that sweet novel of his, *Paul et Virginie,* wouldn't move anyone today."

"Alas no: Paul would be a banker today, and Virginie would marry the son of a manufacturer of railway tracks. Now here are the famous memoirs of Monsieur de Talleyrand, published, on his orders, thirty years after his death. I'm sure that fellow is still doing diplomacy where he is now, though even Talleyrand won't be able to fool the Devil—for long! Now here's an officer who wielded sword and pen alike, a great Hellenist who wrote in French like a contemporary of Tacitus: Paul-Louis Courier! When our language is lost, Michel, it can be created all over again out of the works of this proud scribe. Here's kindly Nodier, and with him Béranger, a great statesman who wrote his songs in his spare time. And here we have reached that brilliant generation that escaped the Restoration as if it were a seminary, making a great riot in the streets."

"Lamartine," said the young man, "a great poet!"

"One of the leaders of our literature of images, a statue of Memnon that sang so beautifully when touched by sunbeams! Poor Lamartine, after lavishing his fortune on the noblest causes and plucking the harp of the poor in the streets of an ungrateful city, wasted his talent on his creditors, delivered his estate of Saint-Point from the cancer of mortgages, and died of grief at seeing that sacred earth where all his family lay expropriated by a railroad company!"

"Poor poet," Michel echoed.

"Beside his lyre," resumed Uncle Huguenin, "you'll notice Alfred de Musset's guitar: it's never played nowadays, and you have to be an old amateur like myself to delight in the vibrations of its slack strings. We're in the music section of our army now."

"Oh, Victor Hugo!" Michel exclaimed. "Uncle, I hope you consider him among our great captains!"

"In the first rank, my boy, bearing the flag of Romanticism on the bridge of Arcole, victor of the battles of *Hernani*, of *Ruy Blas*, of the *Burgraves*, of *Marion de Lorme!* Like Bonaparte, he was already a general at twenty-five, and defeated the Austrian classics at every encounter. Never, my son, has human thought been brewed more vigorously than in that man's skull, a crucible capable of enduring the highest temperatures known to humanity. I know nothing to exceed him, in antiquity or modern times, for the violence and the richness of imagination. Hugo is the highest personification of the first half of the nineteenth century, and leader of a school which will never be equaled. His complete works have had seventy-five editions, of which this is the last; he is forgotten like the rest, my boy, and hasn't killed enough people to be remembered!"

"Uncle, you have the twenty volumes of Balzac!" exclaimed Michel, standing on a stool.

"Of course I do! Balzac is the first novelist in all the world, and several of his characters have outstripped even Molière's types. In this day and age, he wouldn't have had the courage to write *La Comédie Humaine*."

"Even so, he described some terrible behavior, and how many of his heroes are true to life who wouldn't figure badly among us!"

"Probably you're right," Monsieur Huguenin replied, "but where would he find a de Marsay, a Granville, a Chesnel, a Mirouët, a Du Guénic, a Montriveau, a Chevalier de Valois, a La Chanterie, or women like Madame de Maufrigneuse, Eugénie Grandet, or Pierrette, charming characters of nobility and intelligence and gallantry and charity and candor—these were men and women he copied, not invented! It's true that his misers, the financiers protected by the law, the amnestied thieves would sit for him in great numbers today, and he wouldn't have any difficulty finding a Crevel, a Nuicingen, a Vautrin, a Corentin, or a Gobseck among us!"

"Here's what looks to me," said Michel, moving on to other shelves, "like a considerable author."

"Indeed! That is Alexandre Dumas, the Murat of literature, interrupted by death at his nineteen hundred and ninety-third volume! The most entertaining of all storytellers, whom prodigal nature allowed to abuse . . . everything without doing himself harm—his talent, his intelligence, his verve, his energy, even his physical strength when he took the powder keg of Soissons, his birth, his color, France, Spain, Italy, the banks of the Rhine, Switzerland, Algeria, the Caucasus, Mount Sinai, and Naples, especially when he forced entry on the Spéronare! What an astonishing personality! It's believed he would have reached his two thousandth volume if he hadn't been poisoned in the prime of life, eating a dish he had just invented."

"What a pity!" said Michel. "And this dreadful accident claimed no other victims?"

"Oh yes, unfortunately, among others Jules Janin, a critic of the period who wrote Latin themes at the bottom of his columns. It was at a reconciliation dinner Dumas was giving him. And with them also perished a young writer, Monselet, who has left us a masterpiece, unfinished alas, the *Dictionnaire des Gourmets,* forty-five volumes and he only got as far as *L*—for *larding.*"

"A shame," said Michel, "it certainly sounds promising."

"Now here is Frédéric Soulié, a brave soldier, good for a quick turn, and capable of seizing a desperate position, and Gozlan, a Captain of the Hussars, and Mérimée, a dressing-room General, and Sainte-Beuve, a Quartermaster General, in charge of supplies, and Arago, a learned officer in the engineers, who has managed to be forgiven for his knowledge. Look, Michel, here are the works of George Sand, a wonderful genius, one of the greatest writers of France, finally decorated in 1859 and giving her cross to her son to wear for her."

"What are these forbidding-looking books?" asked Michel, pointing to a long row of volumes concealed by the cornice.

"Move on quickly, my child; that's the row of philosophers, Cousin, Pierre Leroux, Dumoulin, and so many more; but since philosophy is a matter of fashion, you won't be surprised that it's no longer read."

"And who is this?"

"Renan. An archaeologist who caused a stir; he tried to deny the Divinity of Christ, and died thunderstruck in 1892."

"And this one over here?"

"This one's a journalist, an economist, a ubiquist, an artillery General noisier than he was brilliant, by the name of Girardin."

"Wasn't he an atheist?"

"Not in the least; he believed in himself. Now look over here, a bold fellow, a man who would have invented the French language all over again if need be, and would be a classic today, if people still attended his classes: Louis Veuillot, the most vigorous champion the Roman Church ever had, and who died excommunicate, to his amazement. There's Guizot, an austere historian who in his spare time diverted himself by compromising the Orléans claim to the throne. And you see this enormous compilation? This is the only *True and Authentic History of the Revolution and of the Empire*, published in 1895 by order of the government to put an end to the various uncertainties which dismayed this part of our history. Thiers's chronicles were ransacked for this work."

"Oh!" cried Michel, "here are some fellows who look young and eager."

"Right you are; that's the light cavalry of 1860, brilliant, bold, noisy, overleaping prejudices like fences, dismissing the proprieties like barriers, falling, getting up again, and running all the faster, breaking their necks and fighting none the worse for it! Here's the masterpiece of the period, *Madame Bovary,* and Noriac's *Bêtise humaine,* a vast subject he couldn't quite encompass; and here are the rest, Assollant, Aurevilly, Baudelaire, Paradol, Scholl, strapping fellows you have to watch out for no matter what, for they're likely to shoot you in the legs . . ."

"But only with gunpowder," Michel concluded.

"Gunpowder mixed with salt, and that can sting. Now here's a fellow who has no lack of talent, a real mascot of the troupe."

"Edmond About?"

"Yes! He flattered himself—or his public flattered him—he was going to begin Voltaire all over again, and in time he reached as far as his ankle; unfortunately in 1869, just when he was finishing his round of visits for the Académie-Française, he was killed in a duel by a fierce critic, the famous Sarcey."

"If this hadn't happened, would he have gone far?"

"Never far enough," answered Uncle Huguenin. "Now these, my boy, are the principal leaders of our literary army: over there, the last rows of obscure soldiers whose names amaze the readers of old catalogs; continue your inspection, enjoy yourself; there are five or six centuries here that ask nothing better than to be glanced at!"

And that was how the day passed, Michel disdaining the unknowns to return to the illustrious names, but encountering odd contrasts, turning from a Gautier whose opalescent style had staled a little to a Feydeau, the licentious heir of Louvet and Laclos, turning back from a Champfleury to a Jean Macé, the ingenious popularizer of science. His eyes leaped from Méry, who produced wit the way a cobbler produces boots, on commission, to Banville, whom his Uncle Huguenin declared to be no more than a word juggler; then he came across Stahl, so scrupulously published by the house of Hetzel, and Karr, a witty moralist who nonetheless lacked the wit to let himself be pilfered, and Houssaye, who having in another life appeared at the Hôtel de Rambouillet, had retained the absurd style and the précieux mannerisms of the place, and Saint-Victor, still flamboyant after a lifetime of a hundred years.

Then he returned to his point of departure; he took up several of these beloved volumes, opened them, read a sentence in one, a page in another, recited from this one only the chapter headings, and from that one only the titles; he inhaled that literary fragrance that rose to his brain like a warm emanation of bygone centuries, shaking hands with all these friends of the past he would have known and loved, had he had the wit to be born sooner!

Uncle Huguenin looked on, delighted by his nephew's pleasure, feeling younger just to watch him. "And what are you thinking now?" he asked him, when he saw Michel standing motionless, apparently in a trance.

"I'm thinking that this little room holds enough to make a man happy for his whole lifetime."

"If he can read."

"I mean that kind of a man."

"You're right, on one condition."

"Which is?"

"That he not know how to write."

"And why is that, Uncle?"

"Because then, my boy, he might be tempted to walk in the footsteps of these great writers."

"What would be wrong with that?"

"He would be lost."

"Oh, Uncle!" Michel exclaimed, "you're going to draw a moral for me!"

"No, for if anyone deserves a lesson here, I'm the one."

"You! But why?"

"For having brought you into the presence of these wild ideas! I've given you a look at the Promised Land, my poor child, and—"

"And you will let me enter, won't you, Uncle?"

"Oh yes, if you will promise me one thing."

"Which is . . ."

"Only to stroll through. I don't want you to be plowing this ungrateful soil! Remember what you are, what you need to do, what I am myself, and this day and age in which the two of us are living."

Michel made no reply but pressed his uncle's hand; and the latter was doubtless on the verge of repeating his tremendous arguments when the doorbell rang. Monsieur Huguenin went to answer it.

CHAPTER XI

A Stroll to the Port de Grenelle

It was Monsieur Richelot himself. Michel flung himself into the arms of his old teacher; a little more and he would have fallen into those Mademoiselle Lucy held out to Uncle Huguenin, who was fortunately standing at his post and thus forestalled that charming encounter.

"Michel!" exclaimed Monsieur Richelot.

"Himself," Monsieur Huguenin reassured him.

"Ah!" exclaimed the professor, "now this is a happy surprise, and an evening which bodes laetanterly."

"*Dies albo nodanda lapillo,*" riposted Monsieur Huguenin.

"As our dear Flaccus says," Monsieur Richelot confirmed.

"Mademoiselle," stammered the young man, greeting the young lady.

"Monsieur," replied Lucy, with a curtsy that was not altogether clumsy.

"*Candore notabilis albo,*" murmured Michel, to the delight of his professor, who forgave this compliment in a foreign tongue. Moreover the young man had spoken accurately; Lucy's entire charm was portrayed in that delicious Ovidian hemistich: remarkable for the luster of her whiteness! Mademoiselle Lucy was about fifteen and perfectly lovely, with long, blond curls falling over her shoulders in the fashion of the day, fresh and nascent, if that term can express about her what was new, pure, and blossoming; her deep blue eyes sparkling with naive glances, her pert nose with its tiny, transparent nostrils, her mouth moist with dew, the almost nonchalant grace of her neck, her cool and supple hands, the elegant outline of her figure— everything enchanted the young man and left him mute with admiration. The young lady was a living poem; he sensed rather than saw her; she touched his heart before delighting his eyes.

This little ecstasy threatened to last indefinitely; Uncle Huguenin realized as much, seated his visitors, managing to shield the young woman from the rays the poet was giving off, and began talking. "My friends, dinner will be served quite soon; let's chat awhile until it comes. You know, Richelot, it's been a good month since I've seen you. How are the humanities going?"

"They're going . . . away," the old professor replied. "I have only three students left in my rhetoric class. It's a turpe decadence! Soon they'll be getting rid of us, and with good reason."

"Getting rid of you!" Michel exclaimed.

"Can it really have come to that?" asked Uncle Huguenin.

"Really and truly," Monsieur Richelot replied. "Rumor has it that the Literature professorships, by virtue of a decision taken in the General Assembly of the Stockholders, will be suppressed for the program of 1962."

"What will become of them?" Michel wondered, staring at the girl.

"I can't believe such a thing," said his uncle, frowning. "They wouldn't dare."

"They will dare," Monsieur Richelot replied, "and it will be for the best! Who cares about Greek and Latin? All they're good for is to provide a few roots for modern science. The students no longer understand these wonderful languages, and when I see how stupid these young people are, I don't know which I feel more intensely, despair or disgust!"

"Can it be possible," asked young Dufrénoy, "that your class is reduced to three students?"

"Three too many," grumbled the old professor.

"And all three of them dunces into the bargain," said Uncle Huguenin.

"First-class dunces!" returned Monsieur Richelot. "Would you believe that just the other day one of them translated *jus divinum* as 'divine juice'?"

"*Divine juice!*" exclaimed Uncle Huguenin, "that's a budding drunkard you have there."

"And yesterday, just yesterday! *Horresco referens*—guess, if you dare, how another one translated this verse from the fourth canto of the *Georgics: immanis pecoris custos* . . ."

"I'd say it was . . . ," offered Michel.

"I blush for it to the tops of my ears," said Monsieur Richelot.

"All right, tell us," replied Uncle Huguenin. "How did he translate that passage in our year of grace 1961?"

" 'Guardian of a dreadful pecker,' " replied the old professor, covering his face.

Uncle Huguenin could not contain a great burst of laughter; Lucy turned her head away, with a smile; Michel watched her sadly; Monsieur Richelot didn't know where to look.

"O Virgil!" exclaimed Uncle Huguenin, "would you ever have suspected such a thing?"

"You see what it is, my friends!" resumed the professor. "Better not to translate at all than to do it like this. And in a rhetoric class! Best to eliminate the whole thing!"

"What will you do then?" asked Michel.

"That, my boy, is another question, but the moment has not arrived for an answer. We're here to have a good time—"

"Then let's have dinner," interrupted Uncle Huguenin.

During preparations for the meal, Michel started a deliciously banal conversation with Mademoiselle Lucy, full of charming nonsense beneath which occasionally gleamed the traces of thought; at fifteen, Mademoiselle Lucy was entitled to be much older than Michel at sixteen, but she did not abuse the privilege. However, apprehensions for the future darkened her pure forehead and solemnized her expression. She gazed anxiously at her grandfather, who epitomized all of life to her. Michel intercepted one of these glances.

"You love Monsieur Richelot a great deal," he said.

"A great deal, Monsieur."

"So do I, Mademoiselle." Lucy blushed slightly at seeing her affection and Michel's meet upon a mutual object; it was virtually a union of her most intimate feelings with those of another! Michel felt the same, and no longer dared look at her.

But Uncle Huguenin interrupted this tête-à-tête with a loud announcement that dinner was served. A neighborhood caterer had brought in a splendid meal ordered for the occasion. The guests took their places at the feast.

A thick soup and an excellent stew of boiled horse meat, a dish much esteemed up to the eighteenth century and restored to honor by the twentieth, contended with the diners' initial appetite; then came a leg of lamb prepared with sugar and saltpeter according to a new method which preserved the meat and added delicate qualities of flavor, garnished with several tropical vegetables now acclimatized in France. Uncle Huguenin's good humor and enthusiasm, Lucy's grace as she served the others, Michel's sentimental frame of mind—all contributed to making this family repast a charming occasion. However prolonged, it still ended too soon, and the heart was obliged to yield before the satisfactions of the stomach.

Everyone got up from the table.

"Now," said Uncle Huguenin, "we must find a worthy ending to this fine day."

"Let's go for a walk!" exclaimed Michel.

"Oh, let's!" Lucy chimed in.

"Where shall we go?" asked Monsieur Huguenin.

"To the Port de Grenelle," Michel replied.

"Perfect. *Leviathan IV* has just docked, and we can have a look at this marvel."

The little group went out into the street, Michel offered his arm to the young lady, and everyone headed for the railroad station.

This famous project of a Paris seaport had at last been realized; for a long while it had not raised much interest; many visited the canal site and were loud in their derision, dismissing the entire venture as a folly. But in the last decade, the incredulous had been obliged to yield to the facts.

Already the capital seemed likely to become something like a Liverpool in the heart of France; a long series of canals and wet docks dug in the vast plains of Grenelle and Issy could accommodate a thousand high-tonnage vessels. In this herculean task, industry seemed to have achieved the extreme limits of the possible.

Frequently during previous centuries—under Louis XIV, under Louis Philippe—this notion of digging a canal from Paris to the sea had been broached. In 1863, a company was authorized to prepare plans, at its own expense, linking Paris to Creil, Beauvais, or Dieppe; but the elevations necessitated many locks and considerable waterways in order to realize such a project; the Oise and the Béthune, the only available rivers in this area, were soon judged inadequate, and the company abandoned its endeavor.

Sixty-five years later, the State returned to the notion, favoring a system already proposed in the last century, a system whose logic and simplicity had caused it to be summarily dismissed at the time; it involved using the Seine, the natural artery between Paris and the Atlantic.

In less than fifteen years, a civil engineer named Montanet cut a canal which, starting on the Plaine de Grenelle, ended just above Rouen, measuring a hundred and forty kilometers in length, seventy meters in width, and twenty meters in depth; this operation produced a bed containing about a hundred and ninety million cubic meters; such a canal would never be in danger of running dry, for the fifty thousand liters per second the Seine produces amply sufficed to fill it. Excavations in the bed of the lower part of the river had opened the canal to the biggest ships. Thus navigation from Le Havre to Paris no longer raised any difficulties.

There existed in France at the time, according to the Dupeyrat Project, a railway network on the towpaths of all canals. Powerful locomotives towed the tugs and transport vessels with no difficulty. This system, greatly enlarged, had been applied to the Rouen canal, and it may readily be imagined how rapidly commercial vessels as well as government shipping sailed up to Paris. The new port had been magnificently constructed, and soon Uncle Huguenin and his guests were strolling on the granite quays, amid a considerable crowd.

There were eighteen wet docks, only two of which were reserved for the government ships assigned to protect the fisheries and the French colonies. Here, as well, were reproductions of armored frigates of the nineteenth century, which the archaeologists admired without quite understanding.

These war machines had ultimately assumed incredible though readily explainable proportions; for a period of some fifty years, there had been an absurd duel between armor and cannonballs, as to which would resist and which would penetrate. Cast-iron hulls became so thick, and cannon so heavy, that ships ended by sinking under their burden, and this result brought to a close this noble rivalry just when cannonballs were about to triumph over armor.

"This was how they fought back then," observed Uncle Huguenin, pointing to one of these iron monsters pacifically moored at the rear of the basin. "Men shut themselves up in these floating fortresses, and then they had to sink the others or be sunk themselves."

"But individual courage didn't have much to do in such machines," protested Michel.

"Courage was outdated, like the cannons," Uncle Huguenin commented with a smile. "Machines fought, not men; hence the impulse to put an end to wars, which had become ridiculous. I could still conceive of battle, in the days when you stood man to man, and when you killed your adversary with your own hands—"

"How bloodthirsty you are, Monsieur Huguenin!" exclaimed Lucy.

"Not at all, my dear, I'm merely reasonable, insofar as reason has anything to do with such things; war once had its raison d'être, but since cannons have had a range of eight thousand meters, and a thirty-six-millimeter cannonball at a hundred meters could pass through thirty-four horses and sixty-eight men, you'll have to admit that individual courage had become a luxury."

"Indeed," Michel commented, "machines have killed bravery, and soldiers have become mechanics."

During this archaeological discussion, the four visitors continued their promenade through the wonders of the commercial docks. Around them rose an entire town of taverns where sailors ate their meals and smoked their pipes. These brave fellows felt quite at home in this mercantile port in the very center of the

Plaine de Grenelle, and they were free to make all the racket they liked. They formed, moreover, a distinct population, not mingling with the inhabitants of the other suburbs, and quite unsociable. It was a kind of Havre separated from Paris by no more than the width of the Seine.

The commercial waterways were connected by cantilever bridges operated at fixed hours by means of the Catacomb Company's compressed-air machines. The water vanished beneath the ships' hulls; most advanced by means of carbonic-acid vapor; not a three-master, a brig, a schooner, a lugger, a coasting vessel which was not fitted with its propeller; wind was no longer a source of energy; it was no longer in use, no longer sought, and old Aeolus, scorned, hid shame-faced in his bag.

It is easy to imagine how cutting through the isthmuses of Suez and Panama had increased long-distance commercial navigation; maritime operations, delivered from monopolies and from the shackles of ministerial brokers, enormously increased; ships multiplied in all forms. Certainly it was a magnificent spectacle, these steamers of all sizes and all nationalities whose flags spread their thousand colors on the breeze; huge wharves, enormous warehouses protected the merchandise which was unloaded by means of the most ingenious machines; some prepared packing materials, others weighed them, some labeled them, still others stowed them onboard; ships towed by locomotives slid along the granite walls; bales of cotton and wool, sacks of sugar and coffee, crates of tea, all the products of the four quarters of the world were heaped up in towering mountains of commerce; many-colored panels announced the ships departing for every point on the globe, and all the languages of the earth were spoken in this Port de Grenelle, the busiest in the world.

The sight of this vast basin from the heights of Arcueil or Meudon was really splendid; as far as the eye could see extended a forest of flag-studded masts; a tide-signal tower stood at the entrance to the port, while at the rear an electric lighthouse, no longer much used, rose into the sky to a height of 152 meters. This was the highest monument in the world, and its lights could be seen, forty leagues away, from the towers of Rouen Cathedral. The entire spectacle deserved to be admired.

"This is all really splendid," said Uncle Huguenin.

"Pulchre sight," echoed the professor.

"If we have neither water nor sea wind," continued Monsieur Huguenin, "here at least are the ships which water bears and the wind drives!"

But where the crowd clustered most thickly, so that it became really difficult to pass through, was on the quays of the largest basin, which could scarcely accommodate the recently docked gigantic *Leviathan IV*; the last century's *Great Eastern* would not have been worthy to be her launch; her home berth was New York, and the Americans could boast of having defeated the British; the ship had thirty masts and fifteen chimneys; of her thirty thousand horsepower, twenty thousand was for the drive wheels and ten thousand for the propeller; railroad tracks made it possible to circulate swiftly from one end of her decks to the other, and in the space between the masts could be admired several squares planted with huge trees, whose shade spread over flowerbeds and lawns; here the elegant passengers could ride horseback down winding bridle paths; soil spread to a depth of three meters over the main deck had produced these floating parks. This ship was a world, and her crossings achieved prodigious results; she came from New York to Southampton in three days; sixty-one meters wide, her length may be judged by the following fact: when *Leviathan IV* docked prow foremost at the quay, rear-deck passengers still had to walk a quarter of a league before they reached terra firma.

"Soon," Uncle Huguenin said, strolling under the oaks, rowans, and acacias of the promenade deck, "soon they'll manage to construct that fantastic Dutch ship whose bowsprit was already at Mauritius when its helm was still in the harbor of Brest!"

Were Michel and Lucy admiring this enormous machine like the rest of this astonished crowd? I cannot say for certain, but they strolled about, speaking in low voices, or saying nothing at all, and staring into each other's eyes; they returned to Uncle Huguenin's lodgings without having seen much, or anything, of the wonders of the Port de Grenelle!

CHAPTER XII

Quinsonnas's Opinions on Women

Michel spent the following night in a delicious insomnia: why bother to sleep? Better to dream wide awake, which the young man did quite conscientiously until dawn; his thoughts touched the ultimate limits of ethereal poetry.

The next morning, he walked through the offices and climbed onto his Ledger. Quinsonnas was waiting for him. Michel shook or rather squeezed his friend's hand but seemed reluctant to speak. When he began dictating, his voice was strangely ardent.

Quinsonnas stared at him, but Michel avoided meeting his eyes. "Something's happened," the pianist reflected. "What a strange expression! He looks like someone who's just come back from the tropics!"

The day passed in this fashion, Michel dictating, Quinsonnas writing, each watching the other on the sly. A second day passed without producing any exchange of thoughts between the two friends.

"Love must be at the bottom of this," the pianist decided. "Let him stew in his sentiments—eventually he'll talk."

On the third day, Michel suddenly interrupted Quinsonnas as he was forming a splendid capital letter. "My friend," he asked, blushing, "what do you think of women?"

"I was right," the pianist congratulated himself, but made no answer.

Michel repeated his question, blushing even more deeply.

"My boy," Quinsonnas replied solemnly, putting down his pen, "our opinion of women, speaking as men, is quite variable. I myself don't think the same thing about them in the morning that I do at night; spring leads me to different thoughts about them from those I have in autumn; rain or fair weather can remarkably alter my doctrine; in short, even my digestion has an incontestable influence on my sentiments in their regard."

"That's not an answer," said Michel.

"My boy, let me respond to one question by another. Do you believe there are still women on this earth?"

"Do I ever!"

"You meet them from time to time?"

"Every day."

"Understand me," the pianist continued. "I'm not talking about those more or less feminine beings whose goal is to contribute to the propagation of the human species, and who will ultimately be replaced by compressed-air machines."

"You're joking."

"My friend, we are speaking quite seriously, but that may still afford some cause for complaint."

"Oh please, Quinsonnas!" Michel exclaimed. "Be serious!"

"Not for one minute. Gaiety is of the essence. I return to my proposition: there are no women left; the species has vanished, like pug-dogs and megatheriums!"

"Please!"

"Allow me to continue, my son; I believe that there were indeed women in the very remote past; the ancient writers speak of them in quite formal terms; they even cited, as the most perfect specimen among them, the Parisienne. According to the old texts and prints of the period, she was a charming creature, unrivaled the world over; in herself she combined the most perfect vices and the most vicious perfections, being a woman in every sense of the word. But gradually the blood grew thin, the race deteriorated, and physiologists acknowledged this deplorable decadence in their texts. Have you ever seen caterpillars become butterflies?"

"Certainly."

"Well," the pianist replied, "this was just the opposite; the butterfly regressed to being a caterpillar. The caressing manner of the Parisienne, her alluring figure, her witty and tender glances, her affectionate smile, her firm yet precise embonpoint soon gave way to certain long, lean, skinny, arid, fleshless, emaciated forms, to a mechanical, methodical, and puritanical unconcern. The waist flattened, the glance austerified, the joints stiffened; a stiff, hard nose lowered over narrowed lips; the stride grew longer; the Angel of Geometry, formerly so lavish with his most alluring curves, delivered woman up to all the rigors of straight lines and acute angles. The Frenchwoman has become Americanized; she speaks seriously about serious matters, she takes life seriously, she rides on the rigid saddle of modern manners, dresses poorly, tastelessly, and wears corsets of galvanized tin which can resist the most powerful pressures. My son, France has lost her true superiority; in the charming century of Louis XV, women had feminized men; subsequently they have switched gender and no longer deserve the artist's gaze or the lover's attention!"

"Don't stop now."

"Yes," Quinsonnas continued, "you smile! You suppose you have the wherewithal to confound me in your pocket! You have your little exception to the general rule ready to hand! Well, you will merely confirm that rule! I maintain my position. And I shall take it even further: no woman, whatever class she belongs to, has escaped this degradation of the race! What we used to call the grisette has vanished; the courtesan, drearier than ever now that she's a kept woman, displays a severe immorality all her own! She is clumsy and stupid but functions with order and economy, so that no man nowadays ruins himself for her! Ruins himself! Please, the word itself is obsolete! Everyone gets rich today, my son, except the human body and the human mind."

"So you claim it is impossible to meet a true woman in this day and age."

"Indeed, under ninety-five years of age, there are none. The last ones died with our grandmothers. However . . ."

"Oh, however?"

"Such things can be met with in the Faubourg Saint-Germain; in this one little corner of our enormous Paris, that rare plant *puella desiderata*, as your professor would say, is cultivated, but only here."

"So," replied Michel, smiling ironically, "you persist in this opinion that woman is a vanished race."

"My son, the great moralists of the nineteenth century already foresaw this catastrophe. Balzac, who knew something about the subject, suggests as much in his famous letter to Stendhal: Woman, he says, is Passion, Man is Action, and it is for this reason that man adores woman. Well, they are both action now, and as a consequence there are no longer any women in France."

"Fine," said Michel, "and what do you think of marriage?"

"Nothing good."

"But beyond that . . ."

"I should be more inclined toward other men's marriages than my own."

"So you'll never marry?"

"No, not until that famous tribunal demanded by Voltaire is convened to judge cases of infidelity—six men and six women, with a hermaphrodite with the deciding vote in case of a tie."

"Now be serious."

"I am being quite serious; such a tribunal would be the only reliable guarantee! You remember what happened two months ago, Monsieur de Coutances brought adultery charges against his wife."

"No!"

"Well, when the magistrate asked Madame de Coutances why she had forgotten her duties, she replied, 'I have such a poor memory!' And was acquitted. And quite frankly, that response deserved an acquittal."

"Leaving Madame de Coutances aside, let's get back to marriage."

"My son, here is the absolute truth on this subject: being a boy, one can always marry; being married, one cannot become a boy again. Between the married state and the bachelor state yawns a dreadful abyss."

"Quinsonnas, what is it you have against marriage?"

"What I have . . . is this: in an age when the family is tending toward self-destruction, when private interest impels each of its members into divergent paths, when the need to get rich at all costs destroys the heart's sentiments, marriage seems to me a heroic futility; in the past, according to the ancient authors, things were quite different; leafing through the old dictionaries, you will be astonished to find such terms as *Lares and Penates, hearth and home, my life's companion,* and so on, but such expressions have long since vanished, along with the things they represented. They are no longer used; it seems that in the past spouses (another word that has fallen into desuetude) intimately mingled their existence; people recalled these words of Sancho Panza: a woman's advice isn't much, but a man would have to be mad not to heed it! And men heeded it. Consider the difference: the husband nowadays lives far from his wife, he sleeps at his club, eats there, dines there, works there, plays there. . . . Madame's life is her own affair, in every sense of the word. Monsieur greets her as a stranger, if he should happen to meet her in the street; from time to time he pays her a visit, turns up on her Mondays or her Wednesdays; sometimes Madame invites him to dinner, more rarely to spend the evening; finally, they meet so little, see each other so little, speak to each other so little and with so little intimacy, that one wonders, quite rightly, how there happen to be so many rightful heirs in this world!"

"More or less true, I suppose."

"Altogether true, my son. We have followed the tendency of the last century, in which people sought to have as few children as possible, mothers apparently vexed to see their daughters too promptly pregnant, and young husbands in despair at having committed such a piece of clumsiness. Hence, in our day and age, the number of legitimate children has singularly diminished to the advantage of the bastards; these already form an impressive majority; they will soon become the masters in France, and will revive the law which forbids any inquiry into paternity."

"Obvious enough."

"Now, the problem, if it is a problem, exists in every class of society; note that an old egotist like me does not blame this state of affairs, he takes advantage of it; but I insist on my point that marriage is no longer the ménage, and that Hymen's torch no longer serves, as once it did, to warm the soup on the stove."

"Therefore," Michel summed up, "if for some improbable, let us say impossible reason you were to decide to take a wife—"

"My dear fellow, I should first of all attempt to make myself a millionaire like everyone else; it requires a great deal of money to lead an existence-times-two; a girl no longer marries unless she has her weight in gold in the paternal coffers, and a Marie-Louise with her wretched dowry of two hundred fifty thousand francs wouldn't find a single banker's son who would have her."

"But a Napoleon?"

"Napoleons are rare, my boy."

"So I see you have no enthusiasm for marrying."

"Not exactly."

"Would you have any for mine?"

"Now we're getting there," the pianist mused, and made no reply.

"Well, what do you say?"

"I'm looking at you," Quinsonnas replied solemnly.

"And . . ."

"And I wonder where to begin tying you up."

"Me!"

"Yes: madman, lunatic—what's happening to you?"

"I'm happy," breathed Michel.

"Reason it out: either you have genius or you don't. The word offends you, so we'll say talent. If you have no talent, you die in poverty à deux. If you have talent, it's a different matter."

"Different how?"

"My boy, don't you know that genius, and even talent, is a disease, and that an artist's wife must resign herself to the role of a practical nurse!"

"Well, I've found—"

"A sister of charity," interrupted Quinsonnas. "There are none. Only cousins of charity now, and cousins once removed!"

Michel persisted. "I've found, I tell you—"

"A woman?"

"Yes!"

"A young woman? A girl?"

"Yes!"

"An angel!"

"Yes!"

"Then let me tell you, my son, pluck her feathers and put her in a cage, otherwise your angel will fly away."

"Listen, Quinsonnas, I'm talking about a young person who happens to be sweet, kind, loving—"

"And rich?"

"Poor! On the brink of poverty. I've only seen her once—"

"That's a good deal! It might be better to have seen her often."

"Don't joke with me, Quinsonnas; she's my old professor's granddaughter; I love her . . . completely; we've talked like friends who've known each other twenty years; I'm sure she'll love me—she's an angel!"

"You're repeating yourself, my son; Pascal says that man is never entirely an angel or a beast! Well, between the two of you, you and your beauty, you provide a furious contradiction!"

"Oh, Quinsonnas!"

"Calm down! *You're* not the angel! Can it be possible—this fellow's in love! Planning at sixteen to do what is still a piece of stupidity at forty!"

"What is still a piece of happiness, if one is loved," the young man replied.

"Enough. Shut up now!" exclaimed the pianist. "Shut up! You're annoying me! Don't add another word or I—"

And Quinsonnas, annoyed indeed, violently slapped the immaculate pages of the Ledger.

It is apparent that a discussion of women and love can have no end, and this one would doubtless have continued till nightfall had there not occurred a terrible accident whose consequences were to be incalculable. By gesticulating so passionately, Quinsonnas happened to knock over the large siphoniform apparatus which provided his multicolored inks. Floods of red, yellow, green, and blue ran like torrents of lava over the pages of the Ledger. Quinsonnas could not restrain a terrible cry; the offices echoed with it. People supposed that the Ledger was falling. "We're lost," whispered Michel.

"You said it, my son," Quinsonnas replied. "The flood is upon us. *Sauve qui peut!*"

But at this moment Monsieur Casmodage and Cousin Athanase appeared in the accounting offices. The banker headed for the scene of the disaster; in his astonishment he opened and closed his mouth, but no words emerged; rage had stifled him!

And with good cause! That marvelous book in which the enormous operations of the banking house were inscribed—stained! That precious treasure of financial affairs, soiled! That veritable atlas which contained an entire world, contaminated! That gigantic monument which on holidays the concierge would show to visitors, ruined! spattered! lost! And its guardian, the man to whom such a task had been entrusted, had betrayed his mandate! The priest had dishonored the altar with his own hands!

Monsieur Casmodage thought all these horrible things, but he could not utter a word. A dreadful silence reigned in the offices.

Suddenly Monsieur Casmodage gestured at the unfortunate copyist; this gesture consisted of an arm extended toward the door with a force, a resolve, a conviction such that no mistake was possible! This eloquent gesture so clearly meant "Get out!" in every human language that Quinsonnas descended from the hospitable summit where his youth had been spent. Michel followed and advanced toward the banker. "Monsieur," he said, "I am the cause—"

A second gesture made by the same arm extended even more emphatically, if possible, sent the reader after the copyist.

Then Quinsonnas carefully removed his canvas cuffs, took up his hat, dusted it with his elbow, put it on his head, and walked straight up to the banker. The latter's eyes were speaking daggers, but he still could not manage to emit a sound. "Monsieur Casmodage and Co.," Quinsonnas remarked in his friendliest tone, "you may think I am the author of this crime, for it is indeed a crime to have dishonored your Ledger. I must not allow you to remain in this error. Like all the evils of this world, it is women who have caused this irreparable misfortune; therefore address your reproaches to our mother Eve and to her stupid husband; all our pain or suffering proceeds from them, and when we have a stomachache, it is because Adam has eaten raw apples. On which note, Good evening."

And the artist left, followed by Michel, while Athanase propped up the banker's arm, even as Aaron did that of Moses during the battle of the Amalekites.

CHAPTER XIII

Concerning the Ease with Which an Artist Can Starve to Death in the Twentieth Century

The young man's position was singularly altered. How many would have despaired in his place, who would scarcely have envisaged the question from his point of view! If he could no longer count on his uncle's family, he felt free at last; he was dismissed, rejected, and he believed he had escaped from prison; "thanked" for his services, it was he who had a thousand thanks to give. His preoccupations did not permit him to know what would become of him. He felt capable of everything, of anything, once he breathed the open air.

Quinsonnas had some difficulty calming Michel down, but he was careful to let such effervescence diminish. "Come to my place," he said to Michel. "You must get some rest."

"Rest? When day is breaking?" Michel objected, making extravagant gestures.

"Metaphorically, day is breaking, I agree," Quinsonnas replied, "but physically, it is growing dark; night has fallen; now we don't want to sleep by starlight—in fact, there is no starlight. Our astronomers are interested only in the stars we cannot see. Come with me, we'll discuss the situation."

"Not today," Michel answered. "You'd only say boring things—I know them all! What can you say that I don't know? Would you tell a slave drunk on his first hours of freedom: 'Friend, now you're going to starve to death'?"

"Right you are; today I won't say anything; but tomorrow . . . !"

"Tomorrow's Sunday! You're not going to spoil my holiday!"

"All right, we're not going to be able to talk at all then."

"Oh yes we will—one of these days."

"Now here's an idea," said the pianist. "Since tomorrow is Sunday, suppose we visit your uncle Huguenin! I'd like to make that good man's acquaintance!"

"As good as done!"

"Yes, and surely you'll allow the three of us to find a solution to the present situation?"

"All right, all right, if all three of us can't find an answer, there isn't one to be found!"

Quinsonnas merely shook his head, without saying another word.

The next day, he took a gas cab early in the morning and called for Michel, who was waiting for him on the curb. He leaped into the vehicle, and the driver started up his motor; it was wonderful to see this machine move so swiftly without any apparent cause; Quinsonnas greatly preferred this mode of locomotion to trains.

It was fine weather; the gas cab moved through the still-sleeping streets, turning corners sharply, ascending slopes with no difficulty, and sometimes riding with a wonderful speed along the asphalt highways. After some twenty minutes, it stopped at the corner of the Rue du Caillou. Quinsonnas paid the fare, and the two friends had soon climbed up to Uncle Huguenin's apartment. When he opened the door, Michel fell on his neck, then introduced Quinsonnas. Monsieur Huguenin received the pianist cordially, asked his visitors to sit down, and immediately offered them some luncheon.

"Actually, Uncle, I'd made other plans."

"What plans, my boy?"

"Plans to take you to the country for the day!"

"To the country! But there *is* no country, Michel!"

"Quite right," echoed Quinsonnas. "Where would you find country?"

"I see that Monsieur Quinsonnas shares my view."

"Completely, Monsieur Huguenin."

"You see, Michel," continued his uncle, "for me, the country, even before trees, before fields, before streams, is above all fresh air; now, for ten leagues around Paris, there is no longer any such thing! We envied London's atmosphere, and, by means of ten thousand factory chimneys, the manufacture of certain chemical products—of artificial fertilizers, of coal smoke, of deleterious gases, and industrial miasmas—we have made ourselves an air which is quite the equal of the United Kingdom's. Unless we were to travel far—too far for my old legs—there's no hope of breathing something pure! If you'll take my advice, we'll stay where we are, close our windows tight, and have our meal right here, as comfortably as we can."

Matters turned out as Uncle Huguenin desired; they sat down at the table; they ate; they chatted about one thing and another; Monsieur Huguenin observed Quinsonnas, who could not help saying to him, at dessert: "My word, Monsieur Huguenin, you have a fine countenance! It's a pleasure to look at you, these days of sinister faces; permit me to shake your hand once again!"

"Monsieur Quinsonnas, I feel I've known you some time; this boy has spoken of you so frequently; I know you are one of us, and I thank Michel for your good visit; he's done well to bring you here."

"Well now, Monsieur Huguenin, if you were to say that it was I who brought Michel, you'd be closer to the truth."

"What is it that's happened then, that Michel should be brought here?"

"Monsieur Huguenin, *brought* is not the word—*dragged* is what I ought to have said."

"Oh!" exclaimed Michel. "Quinsonnas always exaggerates."

"But what is it?"

"Monsieur Huguenin, look at us carefully."

"I am looking at you, gentlemen."

"All right, Michel, turn around so that your uncle can examine you from every angle."

"Am I to be told the motive for this exhibition?"

"Monsieur Huguenin, don't you find something about us that resembles men who have lately been kicked out?"

"Kicked out?"

"Yes, kicked out in the worst possible way."

"You mean some misfortune has befallen you?"

"Good fortune!" Michel broke in.

"Child!" said Quinsonnas, shrugging his shoulders. "Monsieur Huguenin, we are quite simply out on the street, or better still, on the asphalt of Paris!"

"Can it be possible?"

"Yes, Uncle."

"But what has happened?"

"It was like this, Monsieur Huguenin." Quinsonnas then began the story of his catastrophe; his way of telling a story and of considering events, and his own part in them, and his exuberant philosophy drew involuntary smiles from Uncle Huguenin.

"Yet there's really nothing to laugh about," he said.

"Or to cry about," said Michel.

"What will become of you?"

"Don't concern yourself with me," said Quinsonnas, "the point is the child."

"It would be best of all," the young man retorted, "if you talked as if I weren't here."

"Here's the situation," Quinsonnas continued. "Given a boy who can be neither a financier nor a businessman nor an industrialist, how will he manage in a world like ours?"

"That is certainly the question," said Uncle Huguenin, "and a singularly embarrassing one; you have just named, Monsieur, the only three acknowledged professions; I can think of no others, unless one were to be—"

"A landowner," said the pianist.

"Exactly."

"A landowner!" exclaimed Michel, bursting into laughter.

"And he laughs!" exclaimed Quinsonnas. "He treats with unforgivable frivolity a profession as lucrative as it is honorable. Wretch! have you never realized what it is to be a landowner? My boy, it is positively alarming to think of all that this one word contains. When you consider that a man, a person like yourself, made of flesh and blood, born of woman, of a mere mortal, possesses a certain portion of the globe! That this portion of the globe actually belongs to him, that it is one of his properties, like his own head, and frequently even more than that! That no one, not even God, can take from him this portion of the globe which he transmits to his heirs! That he has the right to dig up this portion of the globe, to cultivate it, to build on it as he pleases! That the air which surrounds it, the water which irrigates it—everything is his! That he can burn its trees, drink its streams, and eat its grass, if he chooses! That each day he tells himself: I own my share of this land which the Creator created on the first day of the world; this surface of the hemisphere is mine, all mine, with the six thousand fathoms of breathable air which rise above it, and fifteen hundred leagues of the earth's crust which extend below! For after all, this man is a landowner down to the center of the earth, and is limited only by his colandowner at the antipodes! But, deplorable child, you can never have realized such things to laugh as you do; you've never calculated that a man possessing a simple acre really and truly owns a plot containing twenty billion cubic meters—his own, all his own, whatever there is that can be all his own!"

Quinsonnas was magnificent: gesture, intonation, figure! He became a veritable presence, created an illusion; there could be no mistake: this was the man who had his place in the sun—a possessor!

"Ah, Monsieur Quinsonnas," exclaimed Uncle Huguenin, "you are splendid! You make me long to be a landowner to the end of my days!"

"But isn't it all true, Monsieur Huguenin? And this child sits there and laughs!"

"Yes, I'm laughing," Michel answered, "for I'll never manage to own even a cubic meter of land! Unless chance—"

"What do you mean by *chance*!" exclaimed the pianist. "You use the word without the slightest comprehension."

"What do you mean?"

"I mean that *chance* comes from an Arabic word signifying 'difficult'! Exactly! For in this world there are nothing but difficulties to overcome! And with perseverance and intelligence, victory can be yours."

"Precisely!" replied Uncle Huguenin. "Now what do you say to that, Michel?"

"Uncle, I'm not so ambitious, and Quinsonnas's twenty billion mean nothing to me."

"But," Quinsonnas continued, "one hectare of land produces twenty to twenty-five hectoliters of wheat, and a hectoliter of wheat can produce seventy-five kilograms of bread! Half a year's nourishment at a pound per day!"

"Oh, food, food!" Michel exclaimed, "always the same old song."

"Yes, my son, the song of bread, which is frequently sung to a sad tune."

"So what is it, Michel, that you propose to do?" asked Uncle Huguenin.

"If I were absolutely free, Uncle," the young man replied, "I'd like to put into practice that definition of happiness I once read somewhere, and which involves four conditions."

"And what, without being too inquisitive, might they be?" asked Quinsonnas.

"Life in the open air," answered Michel, "the love of a woman, detachment from all ambition, and the creation of a new form of beauty."

"Well then!" exclaimed the pianist with a laugh, "Michel's already achieved half his program."

"How's that?" asked Uncle Huguenin.

"Life in the open air—he's already been thrown onto the street!"

"Right," agreed Uncle Huguenin.

"The love of a woman?"

"Let's leave that aside," said Michel, blushing.

"As you wish," Monsieur Huguenin teased.

"As for the other two," Quinsonnas continued, "it's a little more difficult. I believe he's ambitious enough not to be utterly detached from all ambition . . ."

"But the creation of a new form of beauty," Michel exclaimed, leaping up with enthusiasm.

"The fellow's quite capable of that," retorted Quinsonnas.

"Poor child," his uncle observed in a rather sad tone of voice.

"Uncle . . ."

"You know nothing about life, yet all your life you must learn how to live, as Seneca says. I implore you, don't yield to fond hopes—you must realize there are obstacles to face!"

"Indeed," continued the pianist, "nothing happens by itself in this world of ours; as in mechanics, you must consider the milieu, you must bear in mind contacts! Contacts with friends, with enemies, with outsiders, with rivals! The milieu of women, of family, of society! A good engineer has to take everything into account!"

"Monsieur Quinsonnas is right," replied Uncle Huguenin, "but let's be a little more specific, Michel; hitherto you have not succeeded in finance."

"Which is why I ask no better than to follow my own tastes and my talents."

"Your talents!" exclaimed the pianist. "At this moment you present the pathetic spectacle of a poet who is dying of hunger and yet nourishes hope!"

"This devil of a Quinsonnas," Michel remarked, "has a nice way of looking at things!"

"I'm not joking, I'm arguing! You want to be an artist in an age when art is dead!"

"Oh, dead!"

"Dead, buried, with an epitaph and a funerary urn. For example: are you a painter? Well, painting no longer exists; there are no more canvases, even in the Louvre; they've been cunningly restored down to the last century—let them turn to dust! Raphael's *Holy Families* consist of no more than an arm of the Virgin, an eye of Saint John; little enough; *The Wedding at Cana* presents the eye with an aerial bow playing a flying violin; which is quite inadequate! Titians, Correggios, Giorgiones, Leonardos, Murillos, Rubenses—all have a skin disease which they contracted by contact with their doctors, and they're dying of it; we have no more than elusive shadows, indeterminate lines, blackened colors in splendid frames! We've let the pictures rot, and the painters too; for there hasn't been an exhibition in fifty years. And a good thing too!"

"A good thing?" inquired Monsieur Huguenin.

"No doubt, for even in the last century, realism made such strides that we can no longer endure it! I've even heard that a certain Courbet, at one of his last exhibitions, showed himself, face to the wall, in the performance of one of the most hygienic but least elegant actions of life! Enough to scare away Zeuxis's birds!"

"Dreadful!" breathed Uncle Huguenin.

"And he was an Auvergnat into the bargain," Quinsonnas continued. "So in the twentieth century, no more painting, no more painters. Are there sculptors, at least? None whatsoever, ever since they planted the Muse of Industry right in the middle of the Louvre courtyard: a vigorous shrew crouching over some sort of cylinder, holding a viaduct on her knees, pumping with one hand, working a bellows with the other, a necklace of little locomotives around her neck, and a lightning rod in her chignon!"

"I must have a look at this masterpiece," murmured Monsieur Huguenin.

"It's well worth the trouble," Quinsonnas replied. "So, no more sculptors! Are there musicians? Michel is quite aware of my opinions on that subject! Is literature your field? But who reads novels? Not even those who write them, judging by their style! No, all that's over and done with, finished, dead and gone!"

"But even so," Michel protested, "alongside the arts there are professions which maintain some contact with them."

"Oh yes, there was a time when you could become a journalist; I grant you that; it could be done when there existed a bourgeoisie who believed in newspapers and went in for politics! But who bothers with politics now? Foreign policy? No, war is no longer possible, and diplomacy is old-fashioned! Domestic policy? Dead calm! There are no parties in France: the royalists are in trade now, and the republicans in industry; there may be a few legitimists attached to the Bourbons of Naples, who support a little gazette to publish their sighs! The government conducts its affairs like a good merchant, and pays its bills regularly enough; they even say it will distribute a dividend this year!

Elections no longer interest anyone; Député-sons succeed Député-fathers, calmly plying their legislators' trade without making much noise about it, like good children doing their homework in their rooms! You'd really suppose that a candidate came from the word *candid*! Faced with such a state of affairs, what's journalism good for? Nothing!"

"All of which is sad but true," replied Uncle Huguenin. "Journalism has had its day."

"Yes, like a discharged soldier from Fontevrault or Melun; and it won't have another. A hundred years ago, we abused our privilege, and we're paying for it now; in those days few enough people read, but everyone wrote; in 1900 the number of periodicals in France, political or otherwise, reached sixty thousand; they were written in every dialect for the instruction of the countryside—in Picard, in Basque, in Breton, in Arabic—yes, gentlemen, there was an Arabic journal, *La Sentinelle du Sahara*, whom the jokers of the day used to call a *journal hebdomadaire*! And all that fine frenzy of newspapers soon led to the death of journalism, for the indisputable reason that writers outnumbered readers!"

"In those days," Uncle Huguenin put in, "there was also the little local paper in which you rubbed along as best you could."

"Doubtless, doubtless," Quinsonnas returned, "but with all its fine qualities, the same thing was true of it as of Roland's mare; the fellows who wrote it so abused their wits that the well ran dry. No one understood anything anymore, among the few who still read; moreover, those estimable writers ended by more or less killing each other off, for there never was such a consumption of slaps and canings; you had to have a strong back and a good cheek to survive. Excess led to catastrophe, and local journalism joined the grand affair in oblivion."

"But wasn't there also criticism," Michel asked, "and didn't criticism support its personnel?"

"I believe it did," Quinsonnas replied. "It had its princes! There were those who had talent and to spare, even spare talents! These Grands Seigneurs had their clientele; some were even willing to set a price on their praises—and such prices were paid! And paid until the moment when an unexpected event radically extinguished the high priests of calumny."

"What event?" asked Michel.

"The application on a grand scale of a certain article of the Civil Code. Any person named in an article was entitled to respond in the same organ with an equal number of lines; the authors of plays, novels, works of philosophy and history began retorting en masse to their critics; each one had the right to so many words, and each one made use of that right! At first, the newspapers tried to resist; they were doomed; then, in order to contend with the protests, they enlarged their format; but the inventors of some machine or other got involved; you couldn't mention anything without provoking a response which had to be printed; and this process was so abused that ultimately criticism was killed on the spot. And with it vanished journalism's last resource."

"Then what's to be done?"

"What's to be done? That's always the question, unless you become a doctor—if you won't have industry, commerce, finance! And even so, devil take me, I think that diseases themselves are wearing out; if the Faculty of Medicine didn't inoculate us with new ones, it would soon have no work to do. I won't even mention the bar—lawyers no longer plead, they compromise; a good transaction is preferred to a good trial; it's faster, and more profitable."

"But it seems to me," said Uncle Huguenin, "that there are still the financial journals."

Yes, but would Michel want to become a stock reporter, wear the livery of a Casmodage or a Boutardin, round off unfortunate periods on pork bellies, alfalfa, or three percents, getting caught out every day in inevitable errors, prophesying events with great aplomb, on the principle that if the prediction doesn't come true, the prophet will be forgotten, and if it does, he will pride himself on his perspicacity, overcoming rival companies for some banker's greater profit, which is worse than mopping his office floors! Will Michel ever consent to that?"

"Of course not! Never!"

"Then I don't see anything except government jobs, becoming an administrator, an official—there are ten million of them in France; figure the chances of advancement, and take your place in line!"

"My word," observed Uncle Huguenin, "maybe that would be the wisest thing."

"Wise but desperate," answered the young man.

"Well then, Michel?"

"In your review of the paying professions," the latter said to Quinsonnas, "you've left one out."

"Which is?"

"That of a dramatist."

"Ah! you want to write for the stage?"

"Why not? Doesn't the theater give you something to eat, to use your frightful phrase?"

"All right, Michel," Quinsonnas replied, "instead of telling you what I think, I'll give you a chance to try it. I'll give you a letter of recommendation to the Editor in Chief of the Entrepôt Dramatique, and you can see for yourself!"

"When do I start?"

"No later than tomorrow."

"Done?"

"Done!"

"Are you serious?" asked Uncle Huguenin.

"Quite serious," Quinsonnas replied. "Perhaps he'll succeed; in any case, in six months—just like now— it will be time to become a government official."

"Now then, Michel, we'll be keeping an eye on you. But you, Monsieur Quinsonnas, you shared this boy's misfortunes. May I ask what you yourself plan to do?"

"Oh, Monsieur Huguenin! Don't worry about me. As Michel knows, I have great plans."

"Yes," the young man observed, "he wants to amaze the age."

"Amaze the age?"

"Such is the noble purpose of my life; I believe I have my business in hand, and first of all I plan to try it out abroad! As you surely know, that is where great reputations are established."

"You'll be gone?" asked Michel.

"For a few months," Quinsonnas replied, "but I'll be back soon."

"I wish you good luck," said Uncle Huguenin, offering his hand to Quinsonnas, who stood up. "And thank you for everything your friendship has done for Michel."

"If the child will come with me now, I'll give him his letter of recommendation right away."

"Gladly!" said the young man. "Good-bye, dear Uncle."

"Good-bye, my boy."

"Good-bye, Monsieur Huguenin," said the pianist.

"Good-bye, Monsieur Quinsonnas, may fortune smile upon you."

"Smile!" exclaimed Quinsonnas. "Better than that, Monsieur Huguenin, I want her to laugh out loud!"

CHAPTER XIV

Le Grand Entrepôt Dramatique

In an age when everything was centralized, thought as well as mechanical power, the creation of a sort of theatrical depository, an Entrêpot Dramatique, was a foregone conclusion; by 1903 a group of practical and enterprising men had obtained the patent for this important company. Within twenty years, however, it passed into government hands and functioned under the orders of a Director General who was a State official.

The Entrepôt Dramatique furnished the capital's fifty theaters with plays of all sorts; some were composed in advance; others were commissioned, sometimes to the requirements of a certain actor, others to satisfy certain concepts. Censorship, confronted with this new state of affairs, tended to disappear, of course, and its emblematic scissors had grown rusty; moreover, from wear and tear they had become quite dull, but the government avoided the unnecessary expense of having them sharpened.

The directors of the Parisian and provincial theaters were State officials, appointed, pensioned, retired, and decorated, according to their ages and their services. The performers drew on the budget, though they were not yet government employees; the old prejudices in their regard were weakening day by day; their métier counted among the honorable professions; they were increasingly to be seen in salon comedies in the best circles; they shared their roles with the guests, and had ultimately become part of society; great ladies now gave cues to great tragediennes, and in certain roles were heard to say lines such as "You far surpass me, Madame, virtue shines in your countenance; I am but a wretched courtesan," and other such courtesies.

There was even one wealthy Sociétaire of the Comédie-Française who made her own children perform chamber plays in her own home.

All of which singularly ennobled the acting profession. The creation of the Grand Entrepôt Dramatique did away with the troublesome necessity of authors; the employees received their monthly salaries—extremely high ones, moreover—and the State collected the theaters' receipts.

Hence the State was in the position of controlling Dramatic Literature. If Le Grand Entrepôt produced no masterpieces, at least it amused docile audiences by harmless works; old authors were no longer performed; occasionally, and as an exception, some work by Molière was put on at the Palais-Royal, with couplets and *lazzi* composed by the actors themselves; but Hugo, Dumas, Ponsard, Augier, Scribe, Sardou, Barrière, Meurice, Vacquerie were eliminated en masse; they had somewhat abused their talents in the past to carry away the public, but in a well-organized society, it was thought best for the public to walk, not run.

Hence matters were now arranged in a methodical fashion, as is suitable in a civilized society; the author-officials lived well and did not tire themselves; there were no more Bohemian poets, those erratic geniuses who seemed eternally to protest against the order of things. Who could complain of this organization which extinguished the artists' personality and furnished the public precisely the amount of literature necessary to its needs?

Occasionally some poor devil, feeling the sacred fire kindled in his breast, attempted to rebel; but the theaters were closed to him by their contracts with Le Grand Entrepôt Dramatique; the misunderstood poet would publish his fine comedy at his own expense, it would remain quite unread and eventually fall prey to those tiny creatures the Entomozoairia, which would ineluctably have been the most learned of their age, had they read all they were given to chew.

So it was to the Grand Entrepôt, lawfully recognized as an establishment of public utility, that Michel Dufrénoy made his way, a letter of recommendation in his hand.

The company's offices were located in the Rue Neuve-Palestro and occupied an old, unused barracks. Michel was shown into the Director's office. The Director himself was an extremely serious man, quite imbued with the importance of his functions; he never laughed or even smiled at the liveliest repartee of his vaudevilles; hence he was said to be quite bombproof; his employees reproached him for his somewhat military leadership; but he had so many people to deal with! comic authors, tragic authors, vaudevillians, librettists, not to mention the two hundred workers in the copying office, and the legion of members of the claque.

For the administration also furnished claques to the theaters, according to the nature of the plays performed; the most learned experts had instructed these carefully disciplined employees in the delicate art of applause, and they had mastered the entire range of its nuances.

Michel presented Quinsonnas's letter. The Director read it through and said: "Monsieur, I am well acquainted with your protector, and I shall be delighted to do him a favor in this regard; he mentions your literary aptitudes."

"Monsieur," the young man modestly replied, "I have as yet produced nothing."

"All the better—in our eyes, that is a virtue."

"But I have some new ideas."

"Of no use, Monsieur! We are not concerned with novelty here; all personality must be dispensed with; you will have to blend into a vast ensemble, which produces collective works, of an average appeal. You will understand that I cannot, in your case, depart from established rules; you must take an examination in order to qualify for a position."

"An examination!"

"Yes, a written composition."

"Very well, Monsieur. I am at your disposition."

"Do you think you are ready for the examination today?"

"Certainly. Right now."

The Director gave orders, and soon Michel was installed at a desk with pen, paper, ink, and a composition subject. He was left alone in the room.

Imagine his astonishment! He had expected to deal with a bit of history, to summarize some product of dramatic art, to analyze a masterpiece of the old repertoire. How childish! His assignment was to imagine a striking effect—a curtain line, say, in a given situation; to compose a song with a witty refrain; and to invent a play on words that would draw a laugh!

Michel took his courage in both hands and set to work.

For the most part, his composition was poor and incomplete—he lacked dexterity, what was still, in the Parisian theaters, called la patte; his curtain line left a great deal to be desired; his refrain was too poetical for a vaudeville; and his pun quite missed the point. Nonetheless, thanks to his protector, he was given employment at eighteen hundred francs; since his curtain line was the least inadequate part of his examination, he was put in the Comedy Division.

This remarkable organization, Le Grand Entrepôt Dramatique, consisted of five major Divisions: (1) high and genre comedy; (2) historical and modern drama; (3) vaudeville, strictly speaking; (4) opera and operetta; (5) reviews, pantomimes, and official occasions.

Tragedy had been eliminated.

Each Division included specialized employees; their nomenclature will explain the mechanism of this great institution, where everything was foreseen, organized, and operated on schedule. A genre comedy or a Christmas review could be produced within thirty-six hours.

Michel was therefore installed in an office in the first Division. Here the talented employees were assigned, one to Exposition, one to Denouements, another to Exits, still another to Entrances; one man was assigned to formal rhymes, when verse was insisted upon; another was responsible for occasional rhymes and prose, in cases of simpler dialogue.

There was also an administration specialty, in which Michel was expected to take part; these highly skilled employees were required to rewrite the plays of previous centuries, either actually copying them or somewhat altering the characters.

It was in this fashion that the administration had just gained an enormous success at the Théâtre du Gymnase with *Le Demi-Monde*, ingeniously transformed; the Baroness d'Ange had become a naive and inexperienced young woman who nearly fell into Nanjac's nets; without her friend, Madame de Jalin (the said Nanjac's former mistress), the trick would have been turned; moreover the episode of the *apricots,* and the description of this world of married men whose wives were never seen, took the house by storm.

Gabrielle had also been reworked, the State having been concerned to spare the feelings of lawyers' wives in some circumstance or other; Julien was about to abandon hearth and home for his mistress, when his wife, Gabrielle, came to him and so vividly described the horrors of a life of infidelity that he abjured his crime for the highest moral reasons, ultimately invoking the family pieties, in words of plaintive address: "O mother of my family, O poet, I love you!"

This play, entitled *Julien,* was actually crowned by the Académie-Française.

Discovering the secrets of this great institution, Michel felt his talents dissolve; yet he had to earn his keep and was soon assigned a considerable task: he was to rework *Nos Intimes* by Sardou.

The wretch sweated blood; he saw the situation clearly between Madame Caussade and her friends, those envious, selfish, and debauched women; he supposed that he could replace Dr. Tholozan by a midwife, and in the rape scene Madame Maurice could keep Madame Caussade's bell from ringing . . . But the denouement! The impossible denouement! No matter how hard he tried, he would never manage to work it out so that Madame Caussade would be killed by that famous fox! He was obliged to give it up and confess his failure.

When the Director learned this result, he was quite disappointed, and it was decided try the young man in the Division of Drama; perhaps he would turn out to have some abilities in this line. After fifteen days of employment in the Grand Entrepôt Dramatique, Michel left the Division of Comedy for that of Drama, which included both historical and modern plays. The former included two sections, quite distinct from each other: one in which actual history was transcribed into the works of good authors; the other in which history was outrageously falsified and denatured, according to this axiom of a great nineteenth-century playwright: *History must be raped if she is to bear a child.* And she was made to bear any number, who themselves bore no resemblance to their mother!

The chief specialists of historical drama were the employees assigned to curtain lines and dramatic effects, especially those of the fourth act; they were handed the situation roughly sketched out and managed to shine it up in no time; also much valued in this Division was the employee assigned to the Grand Tirade, known as the Grandes Dames Special.

Modern Drama included plays in formal dress and those in everyday clothes, even overalls; occasionally the two genres combined, but the administration frowned on such mésalliances, which disturbed the employees' habits and made them far too liable to put in a dandy's mouth the language of a day laborer. And that would have encroached on the specialty of the argot expert.

A certain number of employees were assigned to murders and assassinations, to poisonings and rapes; one of the latter was unrivaled for getting the curtain down at the last possible moment; a second late and the actor, if not the actress, risked being seriously embarrassed. This expert, a good fellow moreover, about fifty years old, father of a family, paid about twenty thousand francs, honorable and honored, had worked variations on this one rape scene for thirty years, with a matchless sureness of touch.

For his first effort in this Division, Michel was assigned the complete reworking of the drama *Amazampo, or the Discovery of Cinchona*, an important play which had first been performed in 1827.

The task was considerable: he had to transform the play into an essentially modern work, an undertaking considerably hampered by the discovery of cinchona, which rather dated matters.

The employees assigned to this project were all at their wits' end, for the work was in very poor condition. Its effects were so worn, its devices so stale, and its construction so weakened by a long retirement in the stacks, that it would have been easier to write an entirely new play; but the administration's orders were incontrovertible: the State wanted to remind the public of this important discovery at a period when periodic fevers were ravaging Paris. Hence the play had to be revised to satisfy contemporary tastes.

The employees' talent and experience prevailed: the thing was a tour de force, but poor Michel counted for nothing in its success; he had contributed not the smallest idea, nor was he able to exploit the situation; he manifested no talent whatever in such matters, and he was declared incompetent.

A report that was anything but complimentary was sent to the Director, and it was determined, after a month of Drama, that Michel was to move down to the third Division. "I'm good for nothing," the young man moaned; "I have neither imagination nor wit! But all the same, what a way to write plays!"

And he despaired, cursing this organization and forgetting that collaboration in the nineteenth century contained in germ the entire institution of the Grand

Entrepôt Dramatique. Here it was merely collaboration raised to the hundredth power.

Michel thus descended from Drama to Vaudeville. Here were collected the funniest men in France; the clerk in charge of rhyming couplets competed with the clerk in charge of punch lines; the section of naughty situations and of blue wisecracks was occupied by a most agreeable young man; the Department of Puns functioned to perfection. Moreover there was a central office of jokes, witty repartee, and preposterous phrases; it fulfilled all the needs of the service in all five Divisions; the administration tolerated the use of a funny line only if it had not been used for at least eighteen months; according to regulations, clerks incessantly ransacked the dictionary and collected all the terms, Gallicisms, and special phrases which, diverted from their usual meaning, produced an unexpected effect; at the company's last inventory, it reported an accumulation of seventy-five thousand plays on words, one quarter of which were entirely new and the rest still presentable. The former, of course, were more expensive.

Thanks to this economy, and this accumulation, the products of the third Division were excellent. When Michel's lack of success in the upper divisions was learned, he was deliberately assigned to an easy role in the confection of vaudevilles; he was not asked to think up new ideas or to invent clever lines; he was provided with a situation and his task was merely to develop it. His first job was a curtain raiser for the Palais-Royal theater; the piece exploited a situation still fresh in the theater and full of the surest effects. Sterne had already sketched it in Chapter Seventy-three of Book Two of *Tristram Shandy*, in the episode of Phutatorius.

The mere title indicated the premise; the play was called *Button Up Your Trousers!*

It may readily be observed how much humor could be drawn from that piquant position of a man who has forgotten to satisfy the most imperious requirement of masculine habiliment. The terrors of his friend introducing him into a salon of the Faubourg Saint-Germain, the embarrassment of the mistress of the house, added to the skill of the actor who was able to play on the audience's fear that at any moment . . . And on the hilarious terror of the ladies who . . . Here was the substance for an enormous success!* Yet Michel, at grips with this highly original idea, was horror-stricken and actually ripped to shreds the scenario which had been entrusted to him. "Bah!" he decided, "I shall not stay another minute in this charnel house! I'd rather starve to death!"

* This play was performed some months later and earned a lot of money. (Author's note)

And he was right! What would he have done? Sink to the Division of Operas and Operettas? Yet he would never have consented to write the mindless verses which the musicians of his day required. And if he sank even further to review, to pantomimes, to official occasions!

But it would be better to be a scene shifter or a painter, and not a dramatic author, producing new stage sets, and nothing else! A great deal in this kind had already been accomplished, what with the advances in machinery—real trees rooted in their invisible crates had been brought onstage, whole flowerbeds, natural forests, and entire structures of stone were built in a few seconds. The ocean was represented with real seawater, emptied each evening before the audience's eyes and renewed the next day!

Did Michel feel capable of conceiving of such things? Did he have it in him to influence audiences, compelling them to leave the contents of their pocketbooks in the theaters' coffers? No, a thousand times no! There was only one thing he could do, clear out of the place. And this he did.

CHAPTER XV

Poverty

During his time at the Grand Entrepôt Dramatique, from April to September, five long months of disappointments and disgust, Michel had not neglected his Uncle Huguenin nor his Professor Richelot.

How many evenings were spent with one or the other, which he counted among the best of his life; with the professor he spoke of the bibliophile; with the bibliophile he spoke not of the professor but of his granddaughter Lucy, and in what terms, with what sentiments!

"I have rather poor eyesight," his uncle remarked to him one evening, "but I do discern, I believe, that you are in love with her!"

"Yes, Uncle, madly in love!"

"Love her like a madman, if you like, but marry her like a wise man, when . . ."

"When . . . ?" Michel asked, trembling.

"When your position in life enables you to do so; succeed for her sake, if not for yours!" To these words Michel made no reply but managed to conceal his rage.

"But does Lucy love you?" his uncle asked him on another evening.

"I don't know," Michel answered. "How could I have any value in her eyes? There's really no reason on earth for her to love me!" And the evening this question was put to him, Michel appeared to be the most wretched man on earth.

Yet the girl never once wondered whether or not this poor boy had a position in life! It never even occurred to her to wonder; gradually she grew accustomed to seeing Michel, to hearing him talk, to expecting him when he didn't come; the two young people spoke of everything under the sun, and the two old men put no obstacle in their way: why keep them from loving each other? They never talked of their love. They spoke of the future. Michel dared not broach the burning question of the present.

"How I'll love you someday," he would say, with a nuance which Lucy understood, a question of time which was not to be answered.

Then the young man flung himself into all his poetical conceptions; he knew he was heard, was understood, and forthwith poured his every aspiration into this young girl's heart. He was truly himself when he was beside her; yet he wrote no verses to Lucy; he was incapable of that, for he loved her too authentically; he understood neither the affiliation of love and rhyme nor the possibility of subjugating his feelings to the requirements of a caesura.

Yet, unbeknownst to him, his poetry was impregnated with his dearest thoughts, and when he recited verses to Lucy, she listened as if she had written them herself; they seemed to respond to some secret question which she dared ask no one.

One evening Michel, looking at her carefully, said: "The day is coming."

"What day?"

"The day when I'll love you."

"Oh!"

And on other occasions, from time to time, he would repeat: "The day is coming." Finally, one fine August evening: "It's come," he said, taking her hand.

"The day when you'll love me," she murmured.

"The day when I love you," Michel answered.

When Uncle Huguenin and Monsieur Richelot realized that the young people had reached this page of the book, they intervened.

"You have read far enough, children; close the book. And you, Michel, now you must work for two."

There was no other engagement party.

In this situation, as will be readily understood, Michel did not speak of his disappointments. When asked how things were going at the Grand Entrepôt Dramatique, he would answer evasively. This was not a satisfactory state of affairs; reality would have to be faced, and he had not yet acquired the habit.

The old men saw no more than this; Lucy divined Michel's sufferings and encouraged him as best she could; but she showed a certain reserve herself, being one of the interested parties in the matter.

Imagine then the young man's profound discouragement, his veritable despair when he found himself once more at the mercy of chance! There came a terrible moment when existence appeared to him in its true aspect, with all its fatigue, its disappointment, its irony. He felt poorer, unworthier, more useless than ever. "What is there for me to do in this world," he agonized, "where I've not even been invited! I must leave!" The thought of Lucy held him. He went to see Quinsonnas, finding him packing a pathetically tiny trunk. Michel described his situation.

"I'm not surprised," Quinsonnas replied. "You aren't made for grand-scale collaborations. What are you going to do?"

"Work on my own."

"Aha!" the pianist responded. "Then you'll stick it out?"

"We'll see. But where are you going, Quinsonnas?"

"I'm leaving."

"Leaving Paris?"

"Yes, and more than that. It's not in France that French reputations are made today; it's foreign products we import, so I'm going to get myself imported."

"But where are you going?"

"To Germany, to stir up those beer drinkers and pipe smokers. You'll hear about me!"

"And you still have your Secret Means?"

"Oh yes. But what about you? You're going to fling yourself into the struggle for existence, which is a good thing. Have you any money?"

"A few hundred francs."

"Not much at all. Now here's a thought—you can have my place: the rent is paid for the next three months."

"But . . ."

"I'd lose it if you didn't take it. I have a thousand francs saved up. Let's divide it."

"Never!"

"Don't be stupid, my boy—I ought to give it all to you, and I'm dividing it. That's another five hundred francs I owe you."

"Quinsonnas . . . ," Michel stammered, tears in his eyes.

"Tears! Well, why not? It's the obligatory stage business for a departure. Calm yourself—I'll be back. All right, give us a hug!"

Michel flung himself into the arms of his friend, who had promised himself he would not be moved, and who fled in order not to break his promise. Michel remained alone. At first he was determined to inform no one of the change in his situation, neither his uncle nor Lucy's grandfather. There was no use burdening them with this additional worry. "I'll work, I'll write," he repeated, in order to harden his resolve. "Others have struggled, when an intransigent age refused to believe in them. We'll see!"

The next day he carried his few possessions to his friend's room and settled down to work. It was his hope to publish a book of useless but splendid poems, and he worked unremittingly, virtually fasting, thinking and dreaming, and sleeping only to dream some more. He heard nothing further about the Boutardins; he avoided streets where he would be likely to meet any of them, imagining that they might attempt to take him back! His guardian never gave him a thought, glad to be rid of a burdensome fool. Michel's only happiness, whenever he left his room, was to visit Monsieur

Richelot. He emerged for no other purpose but came to his old professor's in order to steep himself in the contemplation of the girl, to drink from this inexhaustible spring of poetry. How he loved her! and, it must be confessed, how he was loved! This sentiment filled his existence, nor did he realize that anything else would be necessary in order to live. And yet his resources gradually melted away, though he paid no heed. A visit to the old professor in the middle of October greatly distressed him; he found Lucy sad and sought the reason for her melancholy.

Classes had begun again at the Academic Credit Union; the subject of rhetoric had not been eliminated, it was true, but the end was approaching; Monsieur Richelot had only one student, and if he were to withdraw, what would become of the impoverished old professor? Yet just such an eventuality might occur from one day to the next, and the professor of rhetoric be dismissed. "I'm not concerned for myself," Lucy said, "but I am worried about poor Grandfather!"

"I'll be here, won't I?" Michel declared, but he spoke with so little conviction that Lucy dared not look at him. Michel felt a blush of helplessness rising to his face. And when he was alone: "I promised to be there—if only I can keep my promise! Onward—to work!" And he returned to his room.

Many days passed; many fine notions blossomed in the young man's brain and assumed delightful forms under his pen. Finally his book was done, if such a book can ever be said to be done. He entitled the poems *Hopes,* and indeed his pride required all his poetry in order still to hope.

Then Michel began his great siege of the publishers; it is unnecessary to report the predictable scene which followed each of these harebrained attempts; not one publisher consented even to read his book; such was all his payment for his paper, his ink, and his *Hopes.*

He returned in despair; his savings were dwindling to nothing; he thought of his professor; he sought manual labor, but everywhere machines were advantageously replacing human hands; there were no further resources; in another day and age, he might have sold his skin to some rich boy who wished to avoid conscription; such transactions were no longer possible.

December arrived, the month when everything fell due, cold, mournful, dark, the month which ends the year but not one's sufferings, the month which is generally unwanted in most existences. The most terrifying word in the French language, *misère,* was inscribed on Michel's forehead. His shirts yellowed and gradually fell to pieces, like leaves from the trees at the beginning of winter, and there was no spring to make them grow again. He grew ashamed of himself; his visits to the professor became less frequent, and to his uncle as well; he reeked of poverty; he offered as excuses important work, even absences from the city; he would have inspired pity, if pity had not been banished from the earth in this selfish age.

The winter of 1961-62 was particularly harsh; worse than those of 1789, of 1813, and 1829 for its rigor and length. In Paris, the cold set in on November 15, and the freeze continued uninterrupted until February 28; the snow reached a depth of seventy-five centimeters, and the ice in ponds and on several rivers a thickness of seventy centimeters; for fifteen days the thermometer fell to twenty-three degrees below freezing. The Seine froze over for forty-two days, and shipping was entirely interrupted.

This terrible cold spell was widespread in France and in much of Europe; the Rhone, the Garonne, the Loire, and the Rhine were covered with ice, the Thames frozen as far as Gravesend, six leagues below London; the port of Ostend presented a solid surface which wagons could cross, and carriages traversed the Great Belt on the ice.

The winter's rigors reached as far as Italy, where the snow lay thick on the ground, and Lisbon, where the freeze lasted four weeks, and Constantinople, which was completely snowbound. The extension of these low temperatures had disastrous consequences; a great number of persons died of the cold; it became necessary to suspend all police service; people were attacked nightly in the streets. Carriages could no longer circulate, train service was irregular, and not only did the snow impede movement but it was impossible for the engineers to remain on their locomotives without being mortally stricken by the cold.

Agriculture was especially afflicted by this enormous calamity; in Provence, the vines, chestnut trees, fig trees, mulberry trees, and olive trees perished in great numbers, their trunks splitting vertically with a single terrible crack; even the reeds and briars succumbed to the snow. The year's wheat and hay harvests were utterly compromised.

It is easy to imagine the dreadful sufferings of the poor, despite the State's relief efforts; scientific resources were impotent in the face of such an invasion; though Science had mastered the lightning, suppressed distances, subjugated time and space to its will, placed the most secret powers of nature within the reach of all, controlled floods, and mastered the atmosphere, nothing availed against this terrible and invincible enemy, the cold.

Public charity did somewhat more, but little enough, and poverty attained its ultimate limits. Michel suffered cruelly; he had no fire, and fuel was priceless; his room had no heat whatever. He soon reached the point of reducing his food to the strict minimum and was obliged to resort to the most wretched stopgaps. For several weeks, he lived on a preparation manufactured at the time under the name of potato cheese, a smooth, condensed sort of paste, but even this cost eight sous a pound.

The poor devil then made do with acorn bread, made with the starch of such substances dried in the open air; it was called scarcity bread. But the season's rigor raised the price to four sous a pound, which was still too dear. In January, in the dead of winter, Michel was reduced to eating coal bread: Science had singularly and scrupulously analyzed bituminous coal, which seemed to be a veritable philosophers' stone; it could become diamond, light, heat, oil, and a thousand other elements, for their various combinations have produced seven hundred organic substances. But it also contained in great quantities hydrogen and carbon, those two nutritive elements of wheat, not to mention an essence which produces the taste and fragrance of the most savory fruits. Out of this hydrogen and this carbon, a certain Dr. Frankland had created a sort of bread, which was sold to the needy at two centimes the pound. It must be confessed that one had to be very fastidious to starve to death: twentieth-century science would permit no such thing.

Michel, therefore, did not die. But how did he live?

For cheap as it was, coal bread nonetheless cost something, and when one has no work, two centimes can be found only a certain number of times within a franc. Soon Michel was down to his last coin. He stared at it a long while and began to laugh, though his laughter had a grim ring to it. His head felt bound with iron because of the cold, and his brain was beginning to deteriorate. "At two centimes the pound," he realized, "and at a pound a day, I still have enough for almost two months' worth of coal bread ahead of me. But since I've never given anything to my dear little Lucy, I'll buy her my first bouquet with this last twenty sous." And like a madman, the wretch ran out into the street. The thermometer indicated twenty degrees below freezing.

CHAPTER XVI

The Demon of Electricity

Michel walked through the silent streets; snow muffled the footsteps of the infrequent pedestrians; there was no more traffic; it was dark.

"I wonder what time it is." And the steeple clock of the Hôpital Saint-Louis chimed six. "A clock that measures nothing but sufferings," he thought. He continued on his way, subject to his obsession: he dreamed of Lucy, but sometimes the girl escaped his thoughts, in spite of himself; his imagination failed to hold on to her; he was starving, without realizing it. Force of habit.

The sky glittered with incomparable purity in this intense cold; magnificent constellations stretched as far as the eye could see. Unconsciously, Michel was staring at the Three Kings rising on the eastern horizon in the belt of splendid Orion.

It was a long way from the Rue Grange-aux-Belles to the Rue des Fourneaux, virtually the whole of ancient Paris to be crossed. Michel took the shortest route, turned into the Rue Faubourg-du-Temple, then walked straight along the Rue de Turbigo from the Château d'Eau to Les Halles. From here, in a few minutes, he reached the Palais-Royal and entered the galleries through the magnificent gate that opened at the end of the Rue Vivienne. The gardens were dark and empty; a huge white blanket covered the entire space, without stain or shadow. "It would be a pity to walk on that." And he didn't even realize such a surface would be mainly icy. At the end of the Galerie de Valois, he noticed a brightly illuminated flower shop; he quickly entered and found himself in a veritable winter garden: rare plants, green bushes, freshly picked bouquets, nothing was lacking. Michel's appearance was not promising; the manager of the establishment was mystified by this ill-dressed boy in his flowerbed; they didn't belong together. Michel understood the situation. "Nothing for it," a sudden voice spoke up in his ears.

"What kind of flowers can you give me for twenty sous?"

"For twenty sous!" exclaimed the florist with supreme disdain, "and in December!"

"Just one flower, then," Michel answered.

"All right, we'll give him charity," the florist decided. And he presented the young man with a half-withered bunch of violets. But he took the twenty sous.

Michel left the shop, feeling a singular impulse of ironic satisfaction, after having spent the last of his money. "Here I am, literally without a sou." He smiled, though his eyes remained haggard. "Fine, my Lucy will be pleased with her pretty bouquet!" And he held to his face these fast-fading flowers, inhaling with intoxication their absent fragrance. "She'll be glad to have violets in the middle of winter! Onward!" He reached the quay, crossed the Pont Royal, and made his way through the neighborhood of the Invalides and the École Militaire (it had kept the name, at least), and two hours after leaving his room in the Rue Grange-aux-Belles, he arrived at the Rue des Fourneaux.

His heart was pounding, and he was aware of neither cold nor fatigue. "I'm sure she's expecting me! It's been so long since I've seen her." Then a thought occurred to him. "But I don't want to interrupt their dinner, that wouldn't be right, they'd have to invite me in—what time is it now?"

"Eight o'clock," answered the Église Saint-Nicolas, whose steeple was sharply silhouetted against the sky.

"Oh! by now everyone's finished dinner." He headed for number 49 and knocked gently at the door, hoping to surprise his friends.

The door opened. Just as he began to dash up the stairs, the concierge stopped him. "Where do you think you're going?"

"To see Monsieur Richelot."

"He's not here."

"What do you mean he's not here?"

"He no longer lives here, if you prefer."

"Monsieur Richelot no longer lives here?"

"No! He's left."

"Left?"

"Evicted."

"Evicted!" echoed Michel.

"He was one of those tenants who never can pay the rent at the month's end. He was thrown out."

"Thrown out!" Michel repeated, trembling in every limb.

"Thrown out. Evicted. Dumped."

"Where?"

"I have no idea," replied the State employee, who, in this neighborhood, had not yet risen to the ninth rank.

Without knowing how he got there, Michel found himself back in the street; his hair was standing on end; he felt his head swaying dreadfully. "Evicted," he repeated, "thrown out! Then he too is cold, he too is hungry." And the wretched boy, realizing that all he loved might be suffering, then felt intensely those pains of hunger and cold he had quite forgotten on his own account. "Where can they be? How are they living? The grandfather had nothing, he'll have been dismissed from the school—his one pupil must have left, the cowardly wretch! If I knew him . . . Where are they?" he kept repeating. "Where are they?" he asked some hurrying pedestrian, who took him for a madman. "She must have thought I was abandoning her in her poverty." At this thought, he felt his knees weaken; he was about to fall on the hard-packed snow; by a desperate effort he kept his balance. Yet he could not walk: he ran! Extreme pain produces such anomalies. He ran without purpose, without goal; he soon recognized the buildings of the Academic Credit Union and recoiled in horror. "Oh, Science! Industry!" He returned the way he had come. For an hour, he wandered among the hospices crammed into this corner of Paris—Les Enfants Malades, Les Jeunes Aveugles, l'Hôpital Marie-Thérèse, Les Enfants Trouvés, La Maternité, l'Hôpital du Midi, l'Hôpital de La Rochefoucauld, Cochin, Lourcine; there was no escape from this neighborhood of suffering.

"Yet I don't want to go in here," he kept reminding himself, as if some force were driving him forward. Then he found himself staring at the walls of the Montparnasse cemetery. "Better here," he decided. Like a drunken man he prowled around this plain of the dead. Finally, he came to his senses on the Boulevard de Sébastopol on the Left Bank, passed in front of the Sorbonne, where Monsieur Flourens was still giving his lectures with the greatest success, still ardent, still so youthful. And then the deranged young man realized he was on the Pont Saint-Michel; the hideous fountain, hidden under its crust of ice and quite invisible, presented its most favorable aspect. Michel dawdled, following the Quai des Grands Augustins as far as the Pont Neuf, and there, eyes wild, he began staring at, or rather into the Seine. "Bad weather for despair!" he exclaimed. "A man can't even drown himself." Indeed, the river had frozen over; carriages could drive across it without danger; many booths had been set up on the ice during the day, and here and there bonfires had been lighted.

The splendid river dams of the Seine vanished beneath the mountains of snow; they had been the realization of Arago's great notion in the nineteenth century; dammed, the river would grant the city of Paris, at its lowest level, a power of four thousand horses that cost nothing, and worked constantly. Turbines raised 254 meters of water to the height of 50 meters; now a centimeter of water is twenty cubic meters every twenty-four hours. Thus the inhabitants paid one hundred and seventy times less for their water than in the past; they had a thousand liters for three centimes, and each citizen could use up to fifty liters a day.

Further, the water being constantly displaced in the pipes, the streets were sprinkled by nozzles, and each house, in case of fire, was sufficiently provided with water at a very high pressure.

Climbing up the river dam, Michel heard the muffled sound of the Fourneyron and Koechlin turbines still at work beneath the frozen crust. But here, undecided, he turned back and found himself facing the Institute. He was then reminded that the Académie-Française no longer included a single man of letters; that following the example of Laprade, who had called Sainte-Beuve a bedbug in the nineteenth century, two other academicians subsequently took the name of that little man of genius mentioned by Sterne in *Tristram Shandy*, Book One, Chapter Twenty-one, page 156 of the Ledoux and Teuré edition; now that men of letters were becoming decidedly impolite, members ended by taking only the names of Grands Seigneurs.

The sight of the dreadful dome with its yellowish stripes sickened poor Michel, and he walked past it along the Seine; over his head the sky was cluttered with electric wires passing from one bank to the other and extending like a huge spiderweb as far as the Prefecture of Police.

He walked across the frozen river; the moon projected ahead of his steps his own enormous shadow, which repeated his movements in fantastic parodies. He followed the Quai de l'Horloge, skirting the Palais de Justice; he crossed back on the Pont au Change, whose arches were filled with tremendous icicles; he passed the Tribunal de Commerce, the Pont Notre-Dame, the Pont de la Réforme, which was beginning to sag under its long burden, and continued walking along the quay.

He found himself at the entrance of the morgue, open day and night to the living as well as to the dead; he went in quite mechanically, as if he were looking here for someone dear to him; he stared at the corpses, lying stiff, greenish, and swollen on their marble slabs; in a corner he saw the electric apparatus used to restore life to those waterlogged bodies still harboring some spark of existence. "Electricity again!" he exclaimed, and fled.

Notre-Dame was ahead of him, its windows streaming with light; solemn chanting was audible as

Michel entered the old cathedral. Mass was just ending. Leaving the darkness of the streets, Michel was dazzled: the altar shone with electric light, and beams from the same source escaped from the monstrance raised in the priest's hand. "More electricity," the miserable boy exclaimed, "even here!" And once more he fled, but not so quickly that he failed to hear the organ roaring with compressed air furnished by the Catacomb Company! Michel was going mad; he believed the demon of electricity was pursuing him, and he returned to the Quai de Grèves, entering a labyrinth of empty streets until he came out into the Place des Vosges, where a statue of Victor Hugo had replaced that of Louis XV, and found himself facing the new Boulevard Napoléon IV, which extended to the square where Louis XIV perpetually gallops toward the Banque de France; making a hairpin turn, he came back along the Rue Notre-Dame des Victoires.

On the wall of the street perpendicular to the Bourse, he glimpsed the marble plaque where these words were set in gilded letters:

Historic Marker.
On the fourth floor of this house
Victorien Sardou lived from 1859 to 1862

Michel now stood in front of the Bourse, temple of temples, cathedral of the age; the electric dial showed the time: a quarter to midnight. "The night is frozen too," he mused, as he walked toward the boulevards. The lampposts relayed their cones of intense white light, and transparent signs on which electricity inscribed advertisements in letters of fire glistened on the rostral columns. Michel closed his eyes; he passed through a large crowd leaving the theaters; he reached the Place de l'Opéra and saw that elegant mass of rich people braving the cold in their furs and cashmeres; he skirted the long row of gas cabs and made his escape through the Rue Lafayette, which stretched straight in front of him for a league and a half. "Let's get away from all these people!" he murmured to himself and sprang forward, skidding, hobbling, sometimes falling, getting to his feet bruised but numb; he was sustained by a force that seemed outside himself.

As he walked on, silence and abandonment were reborn around him. Yet far in the distance he saw what looked like a tremendous light; he heard a great noise that sounded like nothing he knew. Nonetheless he continued, finally arriving in the center of a deafening racket, an enormous arena which could easily hold some ten thousand persons, and on the pediment of the building was written in fiery letters:

Electric Concert

Yes, electric concert, and what instruments! According to a Hungarian method, two hundred pianos wired together by means of an electric current could be played by the hands of a single artist! One piano with the power of two hundred! "Away from here, away!" cried the wretch, pursued by this insistent demon. "Away from Paris, perhaps I will find peace!"

And he dragged himself along, as often on his knees as on his feet. After two hours of struggling against his own weakness, he reached the basin of La Villette, and here he lost his way, imagining he had reached the Porte d'Aubervilliers; he followed the endless Rue Saint-Maur, and for an hour after that he skirted the prison of juvenile offenders, at the corner of the Rue de la Roquette. Here a grim spectacle met his gaze: a scaffold was being erected, and an execution would be performed at daybreak. The platform was already rising under the hands of the workers, who were singing at their task. Michel tried to avoid this dreadful sight, but he stumbled over an open crate in which he glimpsed, as he got to his feet, an electric battery! Thoughts flooded his mind, and he understood. Decapitations were no longer in vogue—criminals were now executed by an electric charge. Surely it was a better imitation of divine vengeance.

Michel uttered a final cry, and vanished.

The steeple of Sainte-Marguerite chimed four.

CHAPTER XVII

Et in Pulverem Reverteris

What became of poor Michel during the rest of that terrible night? Where did chance lead his uncertain steps? Did he wander without being able to escape this deadly capital, this accursed Paris? Unanswerable questions.

Apparently he traced endless circles amid those countless streets surrounding the cemetery of Père-Lachaise, for the old burying ground was now in the center of a populous neighborhood. The city extended eastward to the fortifications of Aubervilliers and Romainville. Wherever he had been, by the time the winter sun rose over that great white city, Michel found himself inside the cemetery.

He no longer had the strength to think of Lucy; his ideas were paralyzed; he was no more than a wandering specter among the tombs, and not as a stranger, for he felt at home. He walked up the central avenue and turned right through the sopping lanes of the lower cemetery; snow-laden trees wept over the glistening tombs; the vertical headstones, respected by the snow, were the only ones to offer his eyes the names of the dead. Soon there appeared the ruined funerary monument to Héloïse and Abélard; three columns that supported a broken architrave were still standing, like the Grecostasis of the Roman Forum.

Michel stared blindly; a little farther along he read the names of Cherubini, Habeneck, Chopin, Massé, Gounod, Reyer, in that corner dedicated to those who lived for music and perhaps died of it! He walked on.

He walked past that name encrusted in stone without a date, without carved regrets, without emblems, without pomp, a name still respected by time: La Rochefoucauld.

Then he entered a village of graves as clean as little Dutch houses, with their polished grills at the front and their pumiced thresholds. He felt tempted to go inside. "And stay there," he mused, "resting forever."

These graves, which recalled every style of architecture—Greek, Roman, Etruscan, Byzantine, Lombard, Gothic, Renaissance, Twentieth-century—clustered in a semblance of equality; there was a likeness in these dead—all had turned to dust, whether beneath marble, granite, or black wood crosses.

The young man walked on; gradually he climbed the funereal hill, and aching with fatigue leaned on the mausoleum of Béranger and Manuel; this plain stone cone, without ornaments or sculptures, still stood like the pyramid of Giza and protected the two friends united in death.

Twenty feet away, General Foy kept watch and, draped in his marble toga, seemed to protect them still. Suddenly it occurred to Michel that he should seek among these names; yet not one of them reminded him of those whom time had respected; many, and among these the most elaborately designed, were illegible amid their vanished emblems, carvings of clasped hands now parted, of coats of arms quite ragged now on these graves dead in their turn. Yet he walked on, turned, walked in another direction, leaning against the iron grills, glimpsed Pradier, whose marble *Mélancolie* was falling into dust, Désaugiers, mutilated within his bronze medallion, the tumulary memorial of his students to Gaspard Monge, and the veiled mourner of Etex still crouching at Raspail's tomb.

Climbing farther, he passed a superb monument, its style pure, its marble still proud, with a frieze of naked young girls running and leaping around it, and he read:

To Clairville
His grateful Fellow Citizens

He walked on. Nearby was the unfinished grave of Alexandre Dumas, a man who all his life had searched for the tomb of others.

Now he was in the section of the rich, who still indulged themselves in the luxury of opulent apotheoses; here the names of honest women mingled unconcernedly with those of famous courtesans, those who were able to save up for a mausoleum for their old age; some of the monuments here might easily be taken for brothels. Farther along, he found the graves of actresses on which the poets of the day came to deposit their conceited mourning verses. Finally Michel dragged himself toward the other end of the cemetery, where a magnificent Dennery slept his eternal sleep in a theatrical sepulcher beside Barrière's simple black cross, where the poets encountered each other as in the corner of Westminster, where Balzac emerging from his stony shroud still waited for his statue, where Delavigne, Souvestre, Bérat, Plouvier, Banville, Gautier, Saint-Victor, and a hundred others were no more, even by name.

Lower down, Alfred de Musset, mutilated on his plinth, saw dying at his side the willow he had requested in his gentlest and least sentimental verses. At this moment, Michel's mind cleared; his bunch of violets fell out of his coat. He picked it up and lay it, weeping, on the grave of the abandoned poet. Then he walked higher, higher still, remembering and suffering, and through a clearing in the cypress groves he caught sight of Paris.

Far behind towered Mont Valérien, to the right Montmartre, still awaiting the Parthenon the Athenians would have placed on this acropolis, to the left the Pantheon, Notre-Dame, Sainte-Chapelle, Les Invalides, and farther still the lighthouse of the Port de Grenelle, thrusting its slender beam five hundred feet into the air. Below lay Paris and its jumble of a hundred thousand houses, among which rose the smoke-capped chimneys of ten thousand factories. Farther down, the lower cemetery; from here, some groups of graves seemed like tiny towns, with their streets and squares, their houses and their signs, their churches, even their cathedrals, represented by a more vainglorious grave.

And finally, up above, floated the armored balloons, lightning conductors, which deprived the thunderbolts of any excuse to fall upon the unguarded houses, and wrested all Paris from their disastrous rage.

Michel would have liked to cut the ropes which held them captive and let the city be destroyed under a rain of fire. "O Paris!" he exclaimed with a gesture of despairing rage. "O Lucy!" he murmured, falling unconscious on the snow.

Notes

v *Paul-Louis Courier* (1772–1825): A brilliant polemicist, one of the strongest figures of intellectual opposition to the legitimist and clerical reaction after 1815.

CHAPTER I

10 *Alphonse Karr:* French litterateur, a friend of Verne's publisher Hetzel, known for his satirical verve.

CHAPTER II

19 *Adolphe Joanne:* French geographer, founder of the Guides Joanne, ancestor of the Guides Bleus.

22 *Jean-Baptiste Jobard:* Belgian engineer of French origin, the source of numerous innovations and inventions.

24 *Étienne Lenoir:* Inventor of a gas motor which is the origin of all present-day automobile motors.

CHAPTER III

32 *Thomas Russell Crampton:* English engineer, inventor of one of the first high-speed locomotives.

35 *Joseph Prudhomme:* Character created by Henri Monnier, the type of self-satisfied and sententious bourgeois.

CHAPTER IV

41 *Charles-Paul de Kock:* Prolific author of anecdotal and humorous novels, very popular with a wide public but constantly derided by cultivated circles in the Romantic period.

CHAPTER X

118 *Charles Monselet:* French journalist and gastronome, a friend of Verne's publisher Hetzel.

118 *Frédéric Soulié:* French novelist and dramatic author, a friend of Verne's publisher Hetzel.

118 *Léon Gozlan:* French journalist, at one time Balzac's secretary; a close friend of Verne's publisher Hetzel.

119 *Victor Cousin:* French philosopher, professor of history and philosophy at the Sorbonne.

119 *Pierre Leroux:* One of the chief French socialist thinkers of the nineteenth century.

119 *Émile de Girardin:* French journalist and polemicist.

119 *Louis-François Veuillot:* French Catholic journalist and polemicist.

120 *Claude-Antoine Noriac:* French dramatic author.

120 *Jean-Baptiste-Alfred Assollant:* French author of books for young people.

120 *Paradol (Lucien-Anatole Prévost-Paradol):* French political journalist.

120 *Aurélien Scholl:* French novelist and chronicler, friend of Verne's publisher Hetzel.

120 *Edmond-François-Valentin About:* A brilliant and caustic French writer, friend of Verne's publisher Hetzel.

120 *Francisque Sarcey:* French dramatic critic for forty years.

121 *Jean-Baptiste Louvet de Couvray:* French eighteenth-century novelist and statesman.

121 *Champfleury (Jules-François-Félix Husson):* French critic and novelist, a polemicist for the realist school in art and literature, a friend of Verne's publisher Hetzel.

121 *Jean Macé:* French journalist and educator.

121 *Joseph Méry:* French poet, novelist, and playwright.

121 *P. J. Stahl:* The nom de plume of Hetzel himself, who obviously published him "scrupulously."

121 *Arsène Houssaye:* French critic, journalist, and novelist.

121 *Paul Bins, Comte de Saint-Victor:* French literary critic known for his complex style.

About the Author

JULES VERNE was born in Nantes in 1828, of legal and sea-faring stock, and though educated for the law refused to work seriously at anything but writing. Despite moderate success with plays, Verne did not achieve fame until publication of his novella *Five Weeks in a Balloon* (1853). Coupling a gift for adventure writing with the public interest in technological discoveries, Verne continued with a series of highly successful prophetic science fiction and adventure stories, including *Twenty Thousand Leagues Under the Sea* (1870) and *Around the World in 80 Days* (1873). By the time of his death in 1905 he had written close to one hundred books.

About the Translator

RICHARD HOWARD, born in Cleveland in 1929, is the author of ten volumes of poetry, the third of which won a Pulitzer Prize in 1970, and of many translations from the French. He is a professor of English at the University of Houston and is poetry editor of *The Paris Review*.

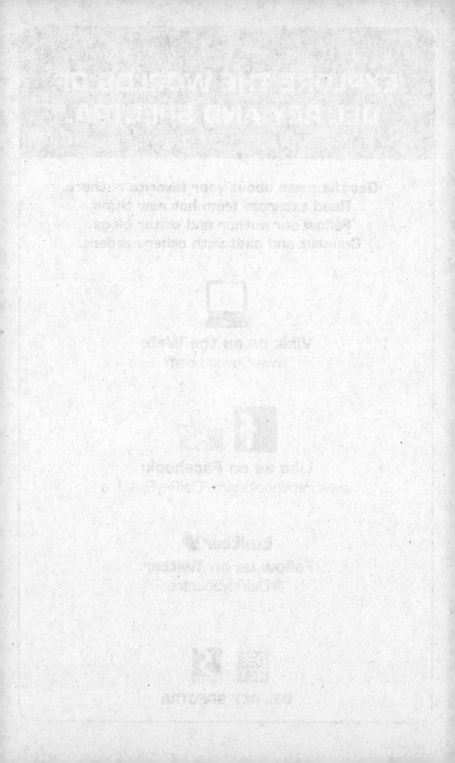